OTHER BOOKS BY KATI

Falling: A Christian Romance Novel

The Crow and The Wind: A little book about a Big God

Out on a Limb of the Family Tree: a novel

The Christmas Closet and Other Works: a holiday book

Signs from God: a novel

The Year of Nine: Where the Rain Begins: a novel

Bernice Branch
2016

To Bernice - One sweet woman!

Bensy and Me

Kathi Harper Hill

By: Kathi Harper Hill

For "Bensy and Me" stories that made the book richer, acknowledgements and thanks to:

Anna Junkins Taylor for the census taker naming a baby.

Mike Watkins for the Redbone Coonhound story.

Nathan Donaldson for the rescue of the calf story.

Pat Lewis for the quote pertaining to if I ain't got nothing to say, I keep talking....

Salvatore Altieri for the use of his name and a story or two. (and the chosen photo for the book cover)

Sylvia Johnson for the bloomers story.

A certain realtor who probably doesn't need to be named for the story of aerial photos.

Marsha Benson, Anna Kate Hill, Betty Jo Holt, Thia Newman: Eagle eyes, all. So much thanks for reading, proofing, correcting and suggestions. I am forever grateful.

What fun the photo shoot was! Thanks to grandmammas, great-aunts, cousins, boyfriends, uncles, daddies, mamas and children who made this possible. A really big thank you to Miss Maggie Parris and Master Sawyer Harper for being the most adorable and cooperative models anyone could ever ask for!

And last, but certainly not least, a thanks to my husband, David: He who has helped paved an open road so I could do all this, by feeding me, working on my neck and shoulders, and being a supreme gofer in all ways. Sometimes, that's the most important job of all.

A special acknowledgement:

The birth announcement for the triplet boys coming into a family with multiple twins and single births, really did appear in the Times-Courier, Ellijay, Georgia in 1911. I changed the name of the father. I didn't have to change the mama's name 'cause she wasn't mentioned.

Authors note:

I've had so much fun writing this book! I hope you have at least half as much fun reading it.

This all started when I was reading an old newspaper article and someone named 'Bensy' was mentioned. I said to my husband right then: "There's a book in that name."

And so there was.

One of the characters in the book is a rather impressive man; at least he is to himself. He uses a lot of very big words, most I'd never heard of.

To help ya'll out, at least those of you who are like me, I included an **'_Uncle Wend Dictionary_'** in the back of the book. Use it if you feel the need.

As always, I appreciate feedback. You can contact me on Facebook, or e-mail: cherokeeirishtemper@yahoo.com, or my blog: kathi-harper-hill.blogspot.com "Everything But The Kitchen Sink".

Just be gentle.

To my identical twin brothers: Because of you I have a fascination about multiple births.

Like arrows in the hand of a warrior are children born in one's youth. Blessed is the man whose quiver is full of them.

Psalm 127: 4 & 5

Bensy and Me

By: Kathi Harper Hill

PROLOGUE:

I knowed Bensy Taylor ever since we was four. We met by the creek bank that's in the rear of Bensy's Granny Taylor's back yard. On the other side of the bank is my Granny Simpson's back yard.

One summer, our two fam'lies had been frequent visitors to our grannies as they was both recently widdered, Bensy's granny just that spring.

Bensy's pawpaw had a tractor turn over on him, and Granny Taylor found him. The doctor told her that he'd never suffered because he'd had hisself a massive heart attack, and that's what caused him to lose control of the tractor in the first place.

I reckon that was supposed to provide some measure of comfort, but I ain't sure it did.

My Granny Simpson was more peaceful about my pawpaw's death, bein as he was a pretty mean drunk for many years of their marriage. Come to think on it, he was about as mean sober. My daddy says he was just surprised Pawpaw *could* die, him bein so mean and all.

When we come in her door that partic'lar day, Daddy hugged her up and asked how she was a'doin.

"Fairly spry, fer a old woman,"she'd said, then told us to hurry and get in, we's lettin all the cold air out.

Granny Simpson had done bought her a winder air conditionin unit and she was treatin it like it owned the place. She said she'd sweated for seventy years in that house, and she wadn't goin to sweat no more. She had used Pawpaw's life insurance money to buy it. She said she didn't think there was a air conditionin unit big enough to cool Pawpaw off where he went.

I reckon she meant Pawpaw was in hell.

I reckon she'd be right.

Anyway, Bensy and me played in that creek all summer. They was always some adult comin to check on us. They wadn't much danger; the creek bein so low that year. But, as my Mama always said, danger can be lurkin at ever corner. Plus, we was only four years old.

Now Bensy and me was thrilled when we started school a few years later, when lo and behold, we was in the same room for first grade. We was fast friends by then, of course, and it was a comfort to find a familiar face. I knowed some of the other younguns in there, too. Our town was not exactly a big city. It was probably a stretch to call it a town, for that matter.

Bensy and me even got to sit together, Bensy bein a *T* and me bein a *S*.

We had a man teacher. His name was Mr. Wright.

He was widdered and a retired college professor. When his

2

wife died, he decided he couldn't stand to live where they had been at it, and bein retired doin nothin on top of that. Him and his wife had plans, but she up and died. He didn't want to do them plans no more.

So he wound up in our little holler teachin first grade.

Bensy's granny took a shine to him the first Sunday he come to our church.

The bad news was, so did my granny.

After that, ever time Bensy and me would meet at the creek, Granny Taylor would holler, "Bensy Taylor, you git in here right this minute!"

And my granny would commence, "Charles Ray Simpson, come here to this house lickity split!"

I reckon they thought misery really did yearn for the company of other poor souls, and they was determined to make Bensy and me as miserable as them. For our grannies had been friends for many years, all the way back to their own childhoods.

Durin recess, we would try to come up with a good plan, but at age six, good plans was hard to come by.

We watched our fam'lies become embarrassed, even at church. Even so, Bensy and me still sat together in the church house. Our mamas said they was the boss of us, not the grannies. They could set wherever they pleased, which was as fer away from each other as they could git.

Even the preacher, who fin'ly got wind of the situation, put his two cents worth in, preachin behind the pulpit. He talked about how we are to love each other as ourselves. He said they couldn't be no fussin in the body of Christ without it hurtin the whole church.

When the preacher said such, our grannies turned and glared at each other.

My Granny Simpson said after church, while we was eatin fried chicken, that it was all Bensy's granny's fault and the Lord would judge her.

My daddy 'bout choked on his cornbread. "Mama," he said, and I felt my whole body cinch up. "How in the world can you say anythang like that when you's as guilty as Miz Taylor?" He throwed down his napkin and stomped out of the dinin room, takin a chicken leg with him.

Of course, Granny Simpson commenced squallin, which, bein only six, I joined right in. My mama picked me up out of my chair and took me to her lap. She looked at Granny Simpson and said, "This is ruinin our lives, Rena. And it's senseless. If you love that man, quit playin mad with Gertie and tell him. And I'd say the same to her. He's not a toy younguns are fightin over. He has a mind. Let him make it up." And with that she toted me out of the room, got her pocketbook, and told my daddy she was ready to go home.

From what Bensy said, their fam'ly was in the same mess.

It got to where we saw each other only at school and Sunday School. We was afraid to even set together durin church meetin, even though our mamas said we could.

The odd thing was, that dang creek near dried up durin all this ruckus.

Thanksgivin was better, such as it was. I don't know if Granny Simpson ever talked to Mr. Wright about her feelins, or if she just sent him hints and dropped by the school when she could scrape up a excuse about me to visit.

I know Bensy's granny was doin the same thing.

I was beginnin to wonder if this mess was ever gonna be cleared up, when Mr. Wright cleared it up hisself.

Christmas vacation time come, and Mr. Wright went back to where he come from for the holidays.

And guess what?

He took Miz Rogers, the school secretary, with him!

She was twenty years younger'n Mr. Wright was, and had never been married.

Until Christmas day.

A'course, none of us knowed such until it was time to start back to school.

Mr. Wright didn't show up. Miz Rogers didn't show up.

Nobody knowed where they was.

Fin'ly, about nine o'clock, the principal's telephone rung and it was Mr. Wright. He explained that him and Miz Rogers had done got hitched and would not be returnin. He said he had plenty of retirement pension and they was gonna take it easy fer a while.

Well, upon hearin that bit of news, Granny Simpson took to her bed for three days.

Granny Taylor left town, herself, and visited Bensy's Aint Susan.

When she come back, Granny Simpson got up outta the bed.

It come a good rain 'cause the weather warmed up some. The creek filled back up right full.

Bensy and me visited our grannies at the same time, and when we met at the creek, nobody yelled at us to get back to the house.

And, although we didn't git to hear it first hand, our grannies made up. They said they was fools, old fools. Their friendship run deep, and I reckon that's why it survived Mr. Wright.

Imagine how bad it would have been if Mr. Wrong had showed up!

Anyhow, this here story is the one Bensy and me will share with our younguns. Cause me and her, we got married right outta high school and lived happily ever after.

So far.

And speakin of younguns…

CHAPTER ONE:

Bensy had been in a bad mood for seven months. I reckon the reason was Bensy was pregnant- again. We done had us two fine younguns. Lilly Ann was three and Monte was two.

As you can imagine, this here was a slip up, and one Bensy was none too happy about. I'd done promised her I was gonna get me one of them vasectomies, but had never quite got up the nerve to do it. So of course, she laid the blame square on my shoulders and would take none for herself. She shore wadn't gonna blame it on that flashy little gown she'd bought at Walmart to celebrate losin all her baby fat. No sir, it was all *my* fault.

I'd been mincin around ever since she'd found out she was pregnant, and was gettin mighty tired of it, too. I mean, lord, how long can a feller put up with such without breakin?

I thought things was pretty bad. So I was tryin to do whatever she asked of me. This was the day for her doctor's appointment. They was concerned because Bensy was a'puttin so much weight on. You can imagine how well *that* set with her.

We hadn't done none of that fancy ultrasound stuff, just the bare minimum, because our insurance wadn't exactly the top of the stack, if you know what I mean.

The nurse checked Bensy's blood pressure and told her it was pretty good, 'considerin'. Bensy glared at me.

I ain't sayin what she weighed, but let's just say I was sure they was somethin wrong with the scales.

They wadn't.

The technician come in and raised up Bensy's shirt and got ready to do the ultra sound. At first the technician was all smilin and chattin, but then she got a funny look in her eye. "I'll be right back. I want Dr. Smith to take a look."

As soon as the door shut, Bensy started squallin. "They's somethin wrong, I know they is! I ain't felt right for a month." She looked at me for the first time in a long time without bein mad. I could see fear instead.

I was feelin pretty fearful myself. Bensy had never been this size before, with either Lilly Ann or Monte. She looked like a hot air balloon she was so swelled up.

The doctor walked in, shook hands with me and said hello to Bensy, pattin her hand. "Let's see what we have here."

He was quiet what seemed like forever. Then he cleared his throat and looked at both of us.

"What's wrong with my baby?" Bensy said, her voice quiverin somethin awful.

Dr. Smith smiled. "As far as I can see, not a thing. It's just that we don't see *a* baby, we see babies."

"Twins?" Bensy asked, her mouth floppin open.

I was as speechless as a mute durin prayer at church. I figured God was gettin even with me for not havin that operation. Our house was goin to be crowded.

"No." Dr. Smith said, grinnin like a jackass in a briar patch. "Looks like triplets to me."

"What!" I cried. "How can I feed five younguns?"

Dr. Smith laughed. "You'll figure it out," he said merrily. "I'm sendin you to a specialist. Three babies at seven months is somethin we don't get caught by surprise about much anymore. Let's get you checked out by someone who knows more about multiple births than I do."

So, bein seven months pregnant, they wanted to see her right away.

On the way, we stopped and got us some dinner at the 'Lucky Diner'. I figured we needed all the luck we could get.

After much hemmin and hawin at the new doctor's, whose name was Kettle, he ordered some other kind of test, but promised it was safe.

When that was over, he called us into his office.

"You are not pregnant with triplets."

"I'm not? How could Dr. Smith make that kind of mistake?" Bensy was startin to sound like the way she'd been talkin to me for six months. It was kind of soothin to hear her aim it somewhere else.

Dr. Kettle smiled. "Because Dr. Smith didn't see the fourth little one hidin behind his brothers."

I swan, I actually got those little black specs and lights you get right before you pass out, which I did once when Junior Johnson hit me with a rock, right smack in the head.

CHAPTER TWO

The next week, I come out of the drugstore, Lilly Ann in tow, with some medicine for Bensy, when Uncle Wend rounded the corner. His real name was Wendall, but he'd always been called Wend because he was so full of hot air.

His face purely lit up at the sight of me. I groaned, and I'm pretty sure I groaned out loud, but that didn't stop Uncle Wend.

"Hey thar, Charlie!" I hated bein called Charlie.

"Hey, Uncle Wend." I wondered if he hated bein called Wend.

"Thar's that cute litlun of yoren." He ruffled Lilly Ann's hair, and she jerked away from him. Lilly Ann hated havin her hair ruffled.

There sure is a lot of hate in this world.

Uncle Wend was a born story teller. Except he was the kind that told you a story whether you was interested in hearin one or not. This left his captive (it always was) audience stupefied or amazed; either way, they was slack jawed, ever time.

For instance, once at my mama's birthday dinner he commenced on a tale about somebody robbin their house and stealin the sterlin silver him and Marveena (that's his wife) got for a weddin present. But this here is the way he told it:

"When we arrived back to our abode after a lovely evenin of dinin out, a burglar of low esteem was absquatulatin with our silver. As he snooved around a corner, Miz Cobb from next door observed he was rather short of stature and was totin a bumbershoot underneath his left appendage."

If that kind of sentence *don't* leave you slack jawed, then I don't know what kind would.

Anyhow, he set in, "I been to the doctor with the gout and there was a ego maniacal hypochondriacal s. o. - "

"Uncle Wend!" I put my hand up to stop him, glancin down at Lilly Ann, who sure 'nuff, was slack jawed.

"Oh, I beg pardon. What I meant to say-"

I shook my head vigorously and plowed through his words, "No, I cain't talk, Uncle Wend." (What I meant was *you* can't talk). "Bensy ain't feelin too spry, and I need to get home with this here Sprite and some medication for her." I glanced down at the poke I was carryin.

His face broke out in a huge grin. He grabbed the hand I was holdin out and begin pumpin it so furiously I thought water would surely start squirtin out my ears at any moment.

"You rascal, you!" He exclaimed, pumpin even harder. "Congratulations! I done heard you had shot four of 'em out of the ball park!"

I blushed, but also felt that stupid grin cross my face that I got ever time somebody gave me credit for gettin Bensy pregnant with quadruplets. If anybody other than the good Lord should be give credit, I reckon it was Bensy. She's the one what had spit out four eggs instead of the normal one. Unless there was identical twins, triplets or quadruplets in there. My grin begin to fade, and I started feelin sorta dizzy again.

"Uh, well, thanks. I appreciate it, and we need your prayers, Uncle Wend. It's a joy, of course, but there may be medical issues…" I trailed off on purpose, glancin down at Lilly Ann again.

He went all serious and patted me on the back, but didn't let go of my hand. Instead he looked heavenward and begin to pray in a very loud voice.

My eyes got wider instead of shuttin! I had no idey he was gonna do that. Lilly Ann looked up at me and grinned.

Little snot.

"Lord God Almighty, here we are Lord, yore small insignificant creations a'spinnin on this blue and green spec out here in the middle of nowhere. Hear our plea, Lord! Now you know Charlie here has done got Bensy pregnant with four of yore creatures," (that made it sound like they could be any type of animal at all, and I heard a snigger from behind. I turned, and it was Otis, who'd followed us out of the store.) I glared at him and then finally remembered to bow my head. "We don't know, Lord," Uncle Wend continued, "Whuther these younguns will be tetched in the head or what, but we's askin yore favor that they won't. And while I'm at it, please have them look more like the Taylors than the Rutleys (this was Bensy's other side of the family). "Amen!"

By then a right smart amount of folks had gathered, half 'bout to bust a gut from laughin and a few religious crazies who was cryin and near shoutin. I didn't see anybody from our church, but if I had, I have a feelin they'd a'prayed hard and then laughed.

Sometimes, you just can't win.

Next stop was Granny's. She'd promised some special tea brewed just this mornin to help Bensy feel better, and since she knowed Lilly Ann was comin with me, I figured a cookie or two would be in the offer.

I hollered through the screen door, and she hollered back to hold my horses.

She come through the livin room wipin her hands on her apron and unlatched the screen door. Her brow was all furrowed and it looked like she'd been cryin some.

"Granny, why are you lookin so sad?"

"Had a good friend die this mornin, hon. Don't live here no more; reckon you don't remember him." A smile come over her face. "He was the thirteenth of thirteen children. He was born real early, and they called him Peanut." She motioned us to come on through and follow her to the kitchen. "When he was five, the census taker come around and when they got to him, his ma said they hadn't never got around to givin him a proper name, just called him Peanut. The census worker studied on that minute, then said, 'Wahl, I'll name him. Son, you are officially named George Washington.' So that's what they put on his birth certificate and everthang."

I shook my head. "I guess that's one way of namin your kids."

"Yessir," Granny said, "Called him Jack for the rest of his life."

"Jack?"

"That's right."

"Why name him George Washington and then call him Jack?"

Granny shrugged. "I reckon he just took to lookin like Jack."

I decided to change the direction of the conversation before I got more confused. "Well, I'm sorry he died. Are you goin to the funeral home?"

"Law, no. He's done bein buried way over in Alabamy sommers. Viola just called me a little while ago to tell me the news. I ain't goin nowhere." She put a big plate of sugar cookies, just liked I'd predicted, in the middle of the table and set out a glass for Lilly Ann. "Here, honey, have a cookie or two. Baked 'em specially fer ye." She turned to me. "Coffee or sweet milk?"

"Milk, please. You gonna eat with us?"

"I believe I will. Don't usually, this time a day, but maybe it'll perk me up a bit."

"Gwanny," Lilly Ann said, "Do you know we's havin some babies come to our house weal soon?"

Granny smiled and patted Lilly Ann on the arm. "I reckon I do, child. It's right excitin, ain't it?"

Lilly Ann thought for a minute. "I guess. At weast I'll have a wittle sister."

I looked at Granny. We knowed for sure three of the babies was boys, but the fourth was unknown. The doctors never knowed if they was lookin at the same three boys, or if the babies was changin places ever time a ultra sound was done. I wadn't gonna argue with Lilly Ann about statistics at the moment, though.

We talked on for a bit, I got the special tea for Bensy, the milk (and some extra sugar cookies), and me and Lilly Ann went on home.

Tomorrow I had to get back to work full time. I'd been workin as much as possible, but with Bensy's doctor's appointments and all, I'd missed a right smart.

****

When I got home, I couldn't wait to tell Bensy about George Washington called Jack.

Bensy was sittin on the couch with pillows proppin up her back and feet. She had a yellow notepad wedged between her belly and what little room there was left in front of her knees. She had a pen in her mouth and had been thinkin pretty hard when I startled her by walkin through the front door.

"Well, you're deep in thought. I bet you didn't even miss me."

I kissed the top of her head, moved her feet a little to get the pillows out from under them; set down and put her feet in my lap. I started massagin her poor swollen feet and she sighed.

"Oh, that feels so good. Don't stop, whatever you do."

"I charge by the hour. Are you sure?" She nudged me with her foot. "So, what's all the list makin about?" I nodded to the legal pad.

"Baby names. I think I got 'em picked out." I raised an eyebrow, but had already decided she could name the babies whatever she wanted to. After all, this was no normal pregnancy, and I was scared to death for her, although I'd never voiced it.

"Okay. Shoot." I leaned my head back, closed my eyes and continued to rub her feet.

"I really like Paul and John and…" she started.

As she continued my heart started racin. I could do with Paul and John. Even George. But there was *no way* I was gonna name my boy Ringo.

"And Matthew, Mark and Luke."

"Oh. Bible names." I sighed with relief. With Bensy, you just never know. "But that's five names."

She frowned. "I know. What do you think about callin one of the boys John Mark?"

I shrugged. "We live in the south." Double names was common here. "I think that's great. So we got Matthew, John Mark, Luke and Paul." I nodded my head. "I like it."

And I really did.

CHAPTER THREE

I had decided, upon takin quick calculations of my life, that a vasectomy was in order. Even if somethin happened to our present litter-in-waitin, we had two healthy younguns. Plus, they wadn't no way I was gonna put Bensy through another pregnancy, not even for one, much less a herd.

Rumor had it that Jack Spratin was the local n'er do well that did the snippin on all us fellers who wanted no more babies, so I signed up to see him.

My first visit was a consultation. Mabel Simpson was the receptionist, a distant cousin of mine, better suited to library work by the look of her sourpuss demeanor and stern countenance.

Tryin to cheer up the woman, I smiled and asked, "Is Jack Sprat in? And can he eat no fat?"

"Ain't likely." She didn't look up or cheer up none, neither.

A nurse come for me after old Mabel had done everthing but frisk me for money, and we journeyed on down the hall where she stopped and did the usual weight, height, blood pressure and temperature. She then situated me in a office and told me Dr. Jack would be with me in a flash.

I reckoned I'd be the one flashin in here.

I can tell you I was shocked to meet old Jack. This man wadn't chubby or portly, he was downright fat. I feared for the door frame as he come through it.

Now, I ain't got nothin against fat people as a general rule; got plenty of 'em in my own family. But they's somethin unsettlin about a doctor comin in and the first two words you think of are morbid and obese. To beat all, when I stood and shook his hand, he reeked of cigarette smoke.

I was considerin the exit when Dr. Jack spoke up.

"To clarify my position here, I need you to know I am a doctor of psychology, not the medical doctor who will be doin the procedure; if, of course, you are deemed stable."

Well, physician, heal thyself, I reckon.

"What do you mean if I'm stable? You mean my mind?" What in thunder, I was wonderin, gettin a little riled, did one have to do with the other?

"Men can have a lot of mixed up emotions about havin this procedure done. You know, feelin as though they are givin up part of their manhood." He leaned toward me (as best he could). "Do you feel that way, Charlie?"

I hate bein called Charlie.

I leaned right back at him and looked hard into his eyes. "Doc, I have two kids already. My wife is pregnant again. *With quadruplets.*" I held up four fingers. "I think I have done more than enough with my manhood."

"I'll say!" Realizin his over enthusiastic response, he cleared his throat. "Congratulations! And I understand your decision." He squirmed a little. "But considerin the high risk nature of such a pregnancy, are you sure you want it done this quickly?"

"When will I ever else have a chance? I got to be able to help with six kids, make a livin and figger where everbody's gonna sleep in my two-bedroom house. It's now, and I mean now!"

I was gettin het up, so he assured me if my wife was in agreement, it could be done as soon as possible.

Now all I had to do was tell Bensy. I figured two things: One, she'd be overjoyed, which she was, and two, she'd set in on me about how I was supposed to do this a year ago, which I was, and which she did.

CHAPTER FOUR

Bensy's granny come to visit on Tuesday, as Bensy was gettin out less and less.

She informed us Chigger Lloyd had brung her. That explained the faint medicinal odor about her.

"Chigger Lloyd just got outta the hoosegow," Granny informed us.

Well, that was a shocker. I never knowed Chigger to be a unlawful person in any way. I'd never been real close to Chigger Lloyd, who was Bensy's first cousin; mainly because of his smell. He was always tryin out some homemade or store bought cure for chigger bites, none of which worked for him.

They tell that when his mama brung him home from the hospital, she stopped to admire a rosebush in bloom, and by the time she got him in the house, he was eat up with chiggers.

He stayed that way all his life to present. From the tender beginnin of spring to the closin down of autumn, that man was covered in 'em.

They come for him even if he stayed on a cement patio.

So, he was evermore searchin for somethin to give him relief.

I opined that perhaps he had finally snapped from itchin so much. After all, Chigger Lloyd was a big old feller.

They'd called him Chigger until he reached twelve, and as he had already said goodbye to six feet, it was sorta silly to call him somethin so tiny. So they attached his given name to it, and he'd been Chigger Lloyd ever since.

"Whatever did Chigger Lloyd do, Granny?" This made Bensy sit up, (as best she could), snappin to attention.

"Aw, he got aholt of some stuff that some fool sold him. Gar-un-teed him he'd stop itchin." Granny cackled. "I reckon he did! Made him drunkern Cooter Brown." She shook her head. "O'course, Chigger Lloyd, bein the true Baptist he is, ain't never been drunk and didn't know he was then. So he gets in his car to go to Bible Study and John Bailey – they done made him a bonafide deputy- pulls him over and tells Chigger Lloyd he's drunk. Made Chigger Lloyd mad and he hit John upside the head the Word O' God!" Granny cackled some more. "They went to it, and afore it was over, they's on the ground rollin around, gruntin and carryin on like boys. That new po-leece officer, Eric somebody, come a'runnin and hollerin at 'em to stop it, but he wouldn't tetch either of 'em. Finl'y Tom Sutton come outta his store thar on the corner and grabbed 'em both by thur collars and hoisted 'em to thur feet. Right then and thar John arrested Chigger Lloyd for D.U.I. and resistin arrest and molestin a po-leece officer."

"Good lord!" I couldn't help but exclaim. "Was either of them boys hurt? Did Chigger break anythang?"

"Not even wind." Granny said.

Bensy was gigglin so hard she had to go pee.

I'll forever more think about Chigger Lloyd molestin a police officer ever time I see him or John Bailey.

CHAPTER FIVE

Most of us from around here had a job, then we had a *job* of farmin. Some had small endeavors, some much bigger.

My buddy, Ron Summers, chose pretty big. Not only did he have a good sized garden where they sold vegetables from all summer, and put up enough to feed a family of twelve, they also had apple trees from which they sold apples and jellies and such, and layin hens so they had eggs to eat and sell. They had cows, too.

We met for breakfast from time to time, mostly just to catch up on fam'ly and such. I hated to bother Ron much, as he worked three ten hour shifts at a factory twenty miles away to supplement their income, and he always looked tireder'n a hound dog after a hunt.

But I was gettin desperate. I had all these younguns on the way and didn't know how on earth I could support everbody. I figured if Ron could give me some pointers about chickens, gardens and cows, I might just keep us all from starvin to death, at least.

Granny had called and told me she needed to talk to me right away. So, a few days ago I'd gone on over to her house to see what she wanted this time. She was forever more needin somethin nailed, screwed in or out, lifted, toted and the like.

When I got there, she handed me some coffee and sugar cookies, homemade. We sat at the kitchen table. She was all wrapped up in a pullover sweater and a button up front sweater and who knows what else. It musta been eighty-five degrees in the kitchen, so I commenced to take off my flannel shirt. I still had on my long johns, so I finally told her I had to get outta that top. I excused myself and stepped into the bathroom, took off the long john top and put the flannel shirt back on. I hoped that would keep the chances of a heat stroke down.

Granny looked right irritated when I come back in, startin in sayin she was a old woman and froze all the time, and this time a year specially, with snow likely on the ground any minute.

I agreed wholeheartedly and told her I was just hot natured. Which I ain't.

She asked after Bensy and all, and we discussed this. She said we's all on the prayer list at her women's circle that quilted, as well as her church. I thanked her and told her prayers was what would get us through.

After hemmin and hawin, which I have never seen Granny do, she come to the point.

"Now, listen here, Charles. I don't want no smart mouthin back. Just hear me out and say yes and thank ye in the end."

This caused all manner of panickin to commence on my insides. What in the world had this woman up her sleeve for me to do? And *thank* her? Did she have a secret bank account and she wanted to give me a thousand dollars or somethin?

"Granny, what in the world are you a'talkin about?"

"Look here. I got twelve acres of land. Good bottom land that could be clured out by the creek. A old chicken house, ain't been used in fifty years, but you could tar down what's left and start over, I'd pay for the lumber and sech. There's room to fence in a place for some cattle." She slapped her hands on the table. "I don't know why ya'll ain't thought about the future, but them babies is gonner take up a lot of room and the mouths to feed will outnumber yore grocery budget, that's fer shore."

I looked at her. She allowed as how we hadn't been *thinkin* about the future? Good lord!

"Granny, that's all I *do* think about! But I cain't take all this. If I could sell my house in town, maybe I could give you that money for a down payment or somethin."

She rolled her eyes. "And jest whar in tarnation do you think I'd live? I shore as the devil ain't gonna live *here* and be turned into a baby sitter. Lord, I'd be in my grave insidea six months. You tryin to kill me?" She squinted her eyes at me, accusinly. "No sir, what I'll do is make a even swap. I take yore house in town, you take all this. I know it ain't got but four bedrooms, but that's a sight bettern what you got now."

No kiddin. Monte still slept in our walk in closet that I didn't finish because when Bensy got pregnant with him, we needed a nursery.

We had planned on havin just one child.

Laugh if you want, but it ain't very funny.

"You'd do that for us?"

"Why not? Yore mine and about to be in dire straights."

I couldn't help it. Tears formed in my eyes and rolled down my cheeks. "I didn't know what I was gonna do. This might save us."

"Well, stop blubberin. You's still gonner have to figger out where to get money for livestock and the hard labor. I'd turn loose of what I got in the bank, but then if I break a hip or somethin I won't have no cushion to see me through."

She was right, of course. I figured I could get some family to help with the labor part and maybe some teen age boys lookin for extra money. I'd already talked to my boss who said I could work a little overtime here and there.

Maybe, just maybe, there'd be some light at the end of the tunnel.

So anyway, there I was, waitin on Ron Summers to see if he could give me ideas and maybe even prices on chickens and cows.

He was fifteen minutes late, and I was about to leave when

he come in. Ron's a big feller, way over six feet tall, and way over three hundred pounds. To say he has a serious case of dunlop disease is a understatement. He come in pullin up his jeans, because he ain't got no butt to hold 'em up, and they have to fit under his belly. Not much room for a waistband.

As he got closer, I was alarmed at the way the man looked. He hadn't shaved, his eyes was bloodshot, and he had sort of a dazed look about him that suggested he hadn't slept.

He sat down with a huff and threw his cap on the table. His flamin red hair stood straight up all over his head. If I could have counted that high, I could have counted ever freckle on his face, that's how pale he was.

"What happened to you?" I asked. "If I didn't know better, I'd say you're hung over." I knowed that wadn't so, as Ron was a deacon down at the Baptist church passed Granny's house.

He scrubbed his hands over his face and looked at me. "You would not believe what happened to me last night." He shook his head. "Mara (that's his wife) called me while I was still at work night before last. It was nearly seven, so I just clocked out to talk to her and then come on home. She told me Dolly's calf was missin. A'course Dolly was carryin on somethin awful, and Mara was nearly as bad. She'd tried to look some, but her bein pragnent and all, she couldn't go far from the house." He snorted. "And nobody in their right mind would leave them boys alone more'n five minutes if they still want their house to be standin." Mara and Ron have three year old twin boys who are somewhat rowdy. I made a mental note to ask him about that, too. (The multiple birth thing, not the rowdiness, as we was personally familiar with that part. Bensy and me had come and eat supper with them a few months ago, right after mornin sickness left Mara and just before she started gettin big as a barn. When Ron said the blessin over the food, he favored us with a rabbit trail in the middle and prayed unashamedly and fervently for a girl this time, whilst both boys tried to disassemble the very chairs we was sittin in at the time.) "I rushed home and looked as best I could, but it was nearly eight o'clock by then and dark as the inside of a unlit stove. They wadn't no sign of the calf."

He stretched, and I could hear what sounded like ever bone he had crackin and snappin. "We didn't sleep too good, not that we get much of a chance to anyhow. This baby keeps Mara up half the night, and if ain't punchin and kickin, the boys are whinin about needin a drink or the monster under the bed and such." He sighed. "Anyway, I had to work yesterday, too, so it was still dark when I left for work. They wadn't no sign of the calf, and I felt real sorry for Dolly when I milked her, but she had to have some relief." He paused a minute. "Now, Charles, you know how much Dolly means to me. And she done lost that first calf. I couldn't see how I could just let another one go."

It was true. Dolly had been more like a pet to Ron than anything. When she herself was a calf and Ron was a teenager, she followed him so bad she walked right into the house with him and his mama liked to died.

The waitress come and I ordered two scrambled eggs, toast and grits. Ron ordered everthing else.

"So, last night, at one minute to seven, Mara calls and says *Dolly* is missin. Now, I figgered Dolly was wherever the calf was, and I reckoned that was good news." He took a swig of coffee the waitress had poured. "Until I got home. We could hear Dolly way off, bellerin like you wouldn't believe. Mara was cryin, the boys started cryin, sayin, *"Find her Daddy, save her! Poor Dolly!"* So, what was I supposed to do? I got my heavy rain coat outta the closet, for it was thirty-four degrees and spittin snow last night. Did you know that?"

I shook my head no. "I heard the weatherman say it might snow some, but I didn't see it."

"Well, take my word for it. It was the icy kind that stings when it hits you in the face."

The waitress come with our breakfast, and another waitress right behind her, for Ron had ordered so much it took two people to tote it all to the table.

He said a quick blessin, took a mouthful, and set in. We eat in silence for a few minutes.

Ron is a eatin machine. He got three or four times more food

33

than I did, but I swan, he finished before I could. It truly is a sight to behold.

I kept eatin and he resumed his tale.

"Back to what I was sayin. I got all wrapped up, Mara even tucked a scarf around my neck down into my coat. Got a boggin on my head and went on out. The wind was blowin, too, so I felt that snow right off. I stopped at the edge of the pasture and hollered for Dolly, and she answered me quick like. I went over towards the creek and looked down. Way down the hill, on the other side of the creek, stood Dolly and her calf. I shined my light on them, and old Dolly mooed with delight. You remember how steep that hill is goin down to the creek?"

I nodded my head yes. It's just about straight down, endin at the creek. There ain't much flat ground around the water until you get to the other side. Then there's some before the land goes straight up again.

"I didn't have no idey how I's gonna get that calf up that hill. I knowed if I could, Dolly would find a way to foller. So I slipped and slid and got down there to them. The only way I could figger out how to get back up the hill was to put the calf around my neck. He's a bull calf, and he's pretty heavy, but after gruntin and squattin and squirmin, I did it. Dolly was all nervous, checkin him ever few seconds because he bawled like I was killin him. But me and Dolly go way back, so she trusted me, I reckon."

The waitress come and refilled our coffee and laid the bill on the table.

"That bull calf is worth a right smart, too, ain't he?"

Ron waved me off, as if that didn't matter a'tall. Maybe it didn't. "Although I'd been able to jump the creek to get to them, they wadn't no way I could jump again with that calf on my back, so I knowed I's gonna have to wade that cold water. I dreaded it, but went on and started across."

He took a big breath, then blowed it out.

"I's about in the middle of the creek when my pants fell down around my ankles."

I choked a little on my coffee. "What?" I snorted. "Sorry, sorry. How'd you get 'em pulled back up?"

"Charles, I don't know if you've ever noticed, but I am a large man with a large belly. And I had a big old calf wrapped around my neck bawlin his head off and his mama bawlin right behind me. I couldn't pull my britches up! I tried to walk on, takin little steps, you know. But them pants finally just worked their way off my feet and floated on down the stream."

It was all I could do to keep from laughin out loud.

"Now, earlier, when I come home and changed outta my uniform to put on my nice, warm, flannel lined jeans that was now floatin down the creek, I failed to put on any drawers." He leaned in close. "I have yet to find my balls, they crawled so fer up inside of me."

There was a moment of profound silence, but that did it. I started shakin like there was a earthquake, then I howled. I whooped. I nearly fell outta my chair.

The whole restaurant turned around and stared at me, and they was grinnin, too, for that kind of laughter is funny in and of itself.

"I'm afraid to ask what happened next," I said to Ron, wipin tears. "But tell me anyway."

"I set the calf down to chase after my britches. You ever tried to put on wet jeans that are lined in flannel?"

"Cain't say as I have."

"Be thankful."

"Oh, I am. More so by the minute."

"Well, the end of the story is I got my pants on, heaved that calf up the hill and Dolly followed. I put 'em up warm and safe in the barn, told Mara my story, which made her pee her pants she was laughin so hard, then I took a warm shower." He took another swig of coffee. "Sorry I was late. So, what is it you wanted to talk to me about?"

CHAPTER SIX

When I got home from work, it seemed like ever woman in the county was at my house cleanin it. In reality, it was both grannies, both mamas, two first cousins and both of Bensy's best friends.

It had been decided that Bensy didn't need to travel to somewhere else for the baby shower, so the baby shower was comin to her.

I will say our house never looked better. I couldn't believe we even lived there. I asked where the kids was goin to be kept until the next afternoon, because they could demolish ever ounce of work that had been done with the snap of a finger.

"They's spendin the night at my house." Bensy's mama said. "Peter (Bensy's daddy) can keep them while the shower is a'goin on, then the little monsters can come back."

They was up to the last minute stuff when the doorbell rang. It was Tim Parker. Him and his brother owned the big car dealership out on the highway. I hardly knowed him, so I was surprised to see him standin there.

He stuck out his hand. "Mr. Simpson?" I shook his hands and nodded yes. "I'm Tim Parker."

"Yessir, I know you – or at least know who you are." I realized I was standin in the door. "Come in! Be careful though, there's a heap of cleanin goin on. We are havin a baby shower here tomorrow."

He come on in. Several of the women openly stared at him, then smiled and spoke. But you could tell they was all curious, like me.

"Have a seat." He sat on the couch, and I sat in the chair next to him. "Can I help you with somethin?"

"Well, Mr. Simpson, as a matter of fact, I'm hopin I can help you." He fidgeted a little, lookin right nervous. "First off, I want to congratulate you on the special event that is about to happen in ya'lls life."

Bensy come in, shook his hand, looked at me for a clue, none of which I had. She sat down in the recliner, wedgin herself in.

"Thank you," we said at the same time.

"I don't know if you are aware that me and my brother, Tom, is twins."

"No sir, I didn't know that." Tim is short, fat, and baldin. Tom is tall, lanky with a full head of auburn colored hair.

He grinned. "Unless you knowed us growin up, you wouldn't. We are what you call fraternal, and that's why we don't look nothin alike. Do you know if all yours are fraternal?"

I shook my head. Bensy said, "They don't know for sure. It's pretty crowded in here," she patted her tummy, "so they try to count heads and be done. They do know at least three are boys, probably all four."

Mr. Parker blushed at the "crowded" remark, and chuckled a little bit. "Me and Tom have always been fascinated with multiple births. I reckon bein twins is the reason. We'd like to make a proposal to ya'll."

"Okay." I wondered what in the world he was gettin at.

"We'd like to present you with a brand new van, big enough to tote all your younguns safely. But they is a few strings attached, so don't thank me yet. We ask that we are permitted to do a video of ya'll puttin the babies in the van when you bring them home from the hospital, and then again ever year on their birthdays until you ain't drivin it no more."

To say we was stunned is a understatement. I wanted to jump up and kiss him on top of his bald little head. If Bensy coulda got outta that chair quick-like, she'd a done it, for sure. Instead she just started squallin.

"Mr. Parker, I don't know what to say. I mean, that's one of the things that has kept me awake nights, tryin to figger out how in the world we was gonna get our babies home, or anywhere else for that matter." I glanced at Bensy, she was noddin yes. "I cain't thank you enough. The answer is yes."

Mr. Parker broke out in a big old grin. "They's more good news, too. Our older brother, Zeke, owns a gas station out on old highway 53. He wants to give you a gift certificate for $500.00 worth of gas. All he asks is that he put one of them magnetic signs on the side of the van advertisin the station until you use up the $500.00. Then he'll come take it off."

"Sounds fair. Lord knows that would be helpful as all get out!"

By now the women had dropped all pretense of workin and was all standin around with their mouths hangin open.

Lookin at them, I asked Mr. Parker, "Do you want us to keep this confidential for now?"

"Lord, no!" He exclaimed. "Folks can talk all they want." He winked. "Good for business, you know."

He left shortly after that.

God is good, as they say. All the time!

****

The baby shower was near bouts as bountiful. Granny's quiltin club had quilted four baby quilts and would cross stitch a name in the corner of each one, as soon as they was born and we knowed for sure they was all boys. Our church put a thousand dollars in our bank account, to use as we saw fit. Our Sunday School class gave us three months of free diapers. The local grocery store donated a case of baby food, whenever we needed to start usin it. Our pediatrician give us free well baby check-ups for the first six months of their lives. The Youth Group promised free baby-sittin services for a year, and talked excitedly about how they could tag team each other and do whatever we needed doin. Granny's Bible Study group promised a home cooked meal ever night but Fridays for a month. Made my stomach growl. Them women could cook!

And then, of course, there was the usual assortment of booties, onesies, sleepers, hats, receivin blankets, wash cloths, etc. One of Bensy's friends give her a big old laundry basket filled with baby detergent, lotions, fabric sheets, diaper wipes, stuff like that.

The list went on and on.

I ain't never seen so much stuff in my life. And the scary thing was, I knowed it would never be enough. But Lord knowed, it sure was gonna give me some breathin room till I could get the chicken houses in shape and buy a few cows.

CHAPTER SEVEN

On Sunday afternoon, Andy and Lisa Ann Singleton showed up with dinner. We was sure lookin forward to it, as I ain't much of a cook and Bensy was just about done with anything but survivin. Lisa Ann confessed to skippin out on church services after Sunday school and settin in to cookin. "I figger God would approve," she said. I believe she was right.

They even pitched in and helped me clean up the mess, which was almost as good as the food that caused it all.

Then, as is custom when weather permits, me and Andy retired to the front porch. The weather had turned off unusually warm these past few days, and it was a easy sixty-five degrees. One thing led to another, and before I knowed what was happenin, Andy had convinced me to go fishin.

"You're workin too hard, and you're strung up over all this baby business way too much lately. You know Lisa Ann will stay with Bensy, they'll be fine. Our cell phones work out there on the river bank, and we could be back here in a jiffy if need be."

It was great. We fished and gossiped, except when men gossip, it's called catchin up on town business and local news. Bein hottern usual, we started sweatin. Andy looked at me, grinned and said, "I double dog dare you to go swimmin. I *triple* dog dare you to skinny dip."

I looked at him like he was crazy, which he was. I said, "We'd freeze our privates plumb off."

Andy looked right back at me and said, "Well, now, that'll save you some money, won't it?" That's what I get for confidin in him about the vasectomy business.

Finally, the mentality of "I will if you will" won, and we stripped, whoopin and hollerin before we jumped in.

We hadn't been in more'n five minutes, but after doin the manly splashin each other, we decided we couldn't stand it no more. We started to get out until Andy said, "Stop."

Waftin through the still air, we could hear several voices singin, 'Shall We Gather at the River'. Gazin up, we could see a crowd of folks workin their way down the riverbank on the other side. They was all dressed up - men, women and children.   It become obvious they was about to have a baptizin.

"Holy cow." I said softly, struck by awe. I truly was.

"I believe you mean Holy Spirit. He has done showed up. What in thunder are we gonna do?"

I thought for a minute, my teeth chatterin like magpies over corn. "Swim out, as fast as you can. Keep your back turned no matter *what*.   When we get outta the water, grab your stuff and run like the dickens to the woods yonder. We'll stop and get our clothes on there."

We moved in the water as quiet as possible, but I heard a little girl's high pitch voice interrupt the singin, right at '*the beautiful, the beautiful river*' part.

"Mama! Lookie thar!"

The singin stopped and laughter, catcalls, hoots and whistlin commenced. And this from the Pentecostals. Lord knows what woulda transpired if it had been the Baptists.

We hit the bank runnin. Suddenly, ringin loud and clear above everbody else's foolishness was a old woman voice, hollerin out, "Lord help, that's my nephew, Andy! *Andy*! Get some clothes on that fat rear end of yorn! You have done shamed the family!"

"Yes'um!" Andy, the fool, hollered back.

The laughter was even louder. I run like the hounds of hell was after me. As we hit the woods, I grabbed my t-shirt and started dryin off as best I could. "How the heck did your Aint Vernell recognize you from the back like that?" I asked Andy.

"Aw, I got a birthmark on my left butt cheek. Shaped just like a Valentine heart."

Well, that was more'n I ever needed to know about Andy.

I got on my drawers, pants and socks and was hoppin around tryin to get on my shoes when my cell phone rung. It was Bensy. When I managed a strangled 'hello' and got nothin but what I thought was hysterical cryin as a answer, my gut clenched. "What's the matter!" I cried, imaginin her on the floor of the livin room, givin birth to babies, one right after another. I even thought I mighta heard si-reens in the distance.

She finally gasped out, "I hear you mooned the Pentecostals," before she howled some more.

I was gobsmacked, to borry a word from Uncle Wend. "How in tarnation have you heard about this so fast?" I mean, I wadn't even fully dressed yet!

"They was such a clamor goin on Preacher Dunn said they could make one phone call each before they started in on the baptizin."

Preacher Dunn is also our Chief of Police, Monday through Saturday. I guess that habit was deeply ingrained.

"Did the whole congregation see 'Little Charlie', too?" That set her off on another hysterical cackle and I heard Lisa Ann snort three times in succession.

"I'm hangin up, Bensy."

And I did.

CHAPTER EIGHT

Monday come the big day, movin to Granny's and Granny movin into our house.

What she took with her was loaded up on Saturday into a giant movin truck, except for her bed, night stand, coffee maker and a few washcloths and towels. She'd put a few changes of clothes in a basket.

We, on the other hand, had been tryin to pack off and on for a few. The baby shower had slowed us down a right smart.

So on Monday mornin I was havin to shake my tail. Bensy was instructed to stay out of the way, get waited on by her mama, and make sure she kept track of the suitcase she had packed for the hospital. I knowed if that was misplaced we'd be in big trouble.

Several healthy males on both sides of the family showed up, and some friends that could spare a few hours did, too. Uncle Wend called sayin he "Truly regretted missin such a monumental event in the history of our lives," but that he was "feelin right peculiar and was concerned it might be the beginnin of a flu-like virus."

Uncle Wend always felt right peculiar when there was heavy liftin involved.

We had repacked all the baby shower stuff, so it was ready to go, and we loaded up dressers and chests of drawers with the stuff in 'em. I was amazed at exactly how much stuff we had crammed into that little old house in just a few years.

People are pack rats by nature, I reckon.

By Tuesday at around midnight it was a done deal. Bensy's mama had even put sheets and covers on all the beds and had put the dish towels, dishes and glasses and such, right where they belonged.

Monte and Lilly Anne was so tired they went to sleep while my mama was bathin them, and they dropped like stones when put to bed.

Bensy and me went to bed and commenced tossin and turnin. I did the tossin, she did the turnin.

We couldn't decide whose back was hurtin the worst, mine or hers.

Let me stop to say; I was a idiot. Why didn't I realize her 'back pain' wadn't from movin stuff, since she hadn't moved nothin but herself all day?

But the babies; *they* was ready to move.

Out.

Labor had commenced!

****

Bensy stood up to go pee for the fiftieth time that night and let out a little gasp.

"What's the matter?" I felt my heart rate speed up. Bensy is not a gasper.

"I think my water just broke."

I leaped up from the bed like I'd been shot forth and turned on ever light we had in the bedroom.

Sure enough, there she was, wet and lookin a little surprised. "I guess that explains my backache."

I reckoned she was right and went over to the phone to call the hospital. They got more excited than we was and said to come right away. Since she'd only had a back ache and her water had just broke, I figured I could drive her to the hospital. As I mentioned before, my insurance ain't the best in the world, and I knowed a ambulance ride was expensive. Besides, we'd made it there twice before by car, even though Lilly Ann and Monte come pretty quick.

I called Mama and she said they'd be right over to set with Monte and Lilly Ann.

I dressed and loaded up the suitcase in the car while we was waitin on Mama. When I come back into the house, Bensy was doin some serious gruntin.

Stupidly, I asked, "Are you okay, Hon?"

She looked at me with gritted teeth and said, "Oh, I am just hunky dorey, you fool." She gritted her teeth again. "The pains are comin faster."

I called the doctor and he said he was on his way to the hospital and not to panic.

I called *him* a fool under my breath as I hung up.

Then I called Mama again. When they didn't answer I was somewhat relieved until I turned around and looked at Bensy.

"Let's get in the car." I told her. "The younguns are asleep; Mama is on her way and we cain't wait no more."

I could see she was about to protest in spite of her pain, but the headlights from Mama and Daddy's car come shinin through the window. We wasted no time in social niceties, just nodded and agreed we'd let them know somethin as soon as we could. Mama said she'd start callin everbody, which I figured she already had on her cell phone.

About half way to the hospital, Bensy started bearin down. "No! Stop!" I hollered, terrified. I could just see babies start poppin out to the floor board, like a little assembly line.

I grabbed up the cell phone and called the doctor's direct line, which he had given us straight away when Bensy become his patient, due to the delicate situation she was in. I'd never used it before this.

"Hey, Charles. Figured I hear from you. Don't panic. I'm already at the hospital, and we are ready and waitin."

"Doc, she's bearin down in the car. I already seen this twice, and it ain't a pretty sight. When she starts this, they ain't no stoppin and it happens fast."

There was a moment of silence. "I'll call the police and let them know you are comin as fast as you can, and so is Bensy. If I can, we'll do a police escort. Step on it, boy!"

And I did.

****

They was waitin on us, and it was a good thing, too. They rolled that stretcher into the delivery room so fast, Bensy's hair was blowin back like she was in a modelin commercial.

Except I don't think models talk such a way.

The doc was in the delivery room, all scrubbed and jolly. There was three other doctors there, too, and extra nurses and all sorts of extra equipment.

I was scared spitless.

I handed the nurse a list of the names and told her that Bensy had wanted the doc to name each baby from the list as he was born. Save us the trouble later, I reckon.

They slid Bensy from the gurney to the table, she pushed twice more and the first little feller popped out. And thank the good Lord, he was a'screamin.

Bensy laid back and a nurse put a IV in her arm.

The doc proudly said, "We have Matthew Charles, two pounds and three ounces!" Everone clapped hysterically as the nurse worked on Matthew.

In a few minutes, doc announced, "Luke Taylor, three pounds even!"

Then, "John Mark, two pounds and eight ounces!"

Then, "Er, uh, we have a girl!"

"What!" Bensy exclaimed. "Let me see!" She raised up (as best she could) and the doc showed her our daughter.

The nurse said, "Paula?"

Bensy and me nodded our agreement. A middle name could be figured soon.

"Paula, two pounds and two ounces!"

Boy, was I glad *that* was over.

I reckon that's why I fainted dead away.

<u>Birth Announcement in the local paper the followin week</u>:

Mr. and Mrs. Charles (Bensy Taylor) Simpson, their children Lilly Ann and Monte, are proud to announce on April eighth, the birth of quadruplets:
Paula Louise, two pounds and two ounces; John Mark, two pounds and eight ounces; Matthew Charles, two pounds and three ounces; and Luke Taylor, three pounds.

Mother and children are doing well. The daddy, we ain't too sure about!

CHAPTER NINE

Two days had passed by. I had slept at the house for the first time since we'd moved into it, the first bein interrupted by the trip to the hospital, the next two stayin at the hospital with Bensy and the babies. I don't think I coulda tore myself away from them, even if Bensy had wanted me gone. Which she didn't.

But when the doc made rounds the night before and said Bensy could come home the next mornin, I figured it was safe for me to go home and sleep. Which I did.

I'd even made myself a big breakfast and cleaned up my mess. As I started out the door to pick up Bensy and bring her home from the hospital, the phone rang.

It was Mabel from the doctor's office, callin to schedule the vasectomy.

I responded with that news by hiccoughin. It sorta went like this: "When (hic) do you (hic) want to (hic) schedule the sur(hic) sur (hic) surgery?"

"Let me talk, you hiccough. I ain't got all day." She ordered. "Day after tomorrow, 9:00 a.m."

"Day after tomorrow?" I squeaked out.

"Skeered them hiccoughs right outta ya, didn't I?" She didn't have to sound so smug.

"I reckon so. They seem to be gone."

"Dr. Cutts had a cancellation and I heard Bensy had them babies and is doin all right. That so?"

"Yes. She had them day before yesterday. They are all doin pretty good."

"It'll be a while before the younguns get to come home, won't it?"

"Yeah. They have to gain weight."

"Is Bensy home yet?"

"I was headed out the door to go get her when you called."

"Well, your mama or her mama or one of the grannies will be there to help her out. They won't need you no how. Might as well grit your teeth, set your bonnet and get this over with. Who's got Lilly Ann and Monte, God bless 'em?"

"Mama."

"You can just take pain medicine and use a ice pack and stay out of the way. It ain't much recovery as long as you don't lift stuff or exercise." She snorted. "And lord knows you don't exercise."

"Well, I -"

"You better strike while the iron's hot, boy. You don't want Bensy windin up pregnant again. She just might kill you, and that's the truth."

"You're right, I guess. Okay. So I just show up day after tomorrow?"

"That's right. Don't eat or drink nothin after midnight in case they give you a sedative."

"You mean they might *not* give me a sedative?" My voice went up a whole octave.

"I meant general versus local, idiot."

"Oh."

"Well, I ain't got all day to talk to you. I got other stuff to do."

"Wait! Mabel, did you say the doctor's name is *Cutts*?"

I heard her chuckle. "That's right. Mickey Cutts. That's who he is, that's what he does."

Then she hung up. I had to sit down a minute. Somehow or other I hadn't heard his name before. I didn't know if I was gonna throw up or pass out, but turns out I did neither. The phone rung again, this time it was Bensy.

I told her I'd been waylaid by a phone call, and when she asked who, I give her the whole nine yards.

She snickered. "We'll both have our privates outta commission at the same time. Seems sorta fittin, don't it?"

I did not honor that remark with a response a'tall.

I hung up and looked at myself in the mirror.

How come I didn't look no different to be a man whose life had been forever changed, and now was about to go through it maimed?

It seemed like I ort to have at least looked a little wounded.

I reckoned that was about to change in the hands of good old Dr. Cutts.

****

We said a tearful see ya later to the babies. It was a lot harder to leave them there than I had thought about it bein. But, really, I hadn't thought that far. Not sleepin will do that to you.

I was goin back to work (after I recovered from surgery, oh *dear lord*), so startin very soon, Bensy and me would go to the hospital together after we dropped Lilly Ann and Monte off sommers first thing in the mornins. I would visit, go to work, and somebody in the fami'ly would come get Bensy after she nursed, pick up the kids and bring 'em all home until lunch. Somebody would baby sit while somebody else took Bensy back to the hospital to nurse, and bring her home, where she and the kids would stay 'till I got home from work, then somebody would come babysit while Bensy and me visited the babies one last time for the day.

'Somebody' was gonna be awful busy.

We had no idey how long this was goin to go on, but family

and friends swore they didn't care how long it took, they would stand by us and get us to and fro.

All I can say is thank God for family and friends.

CHAPTER TEN

We had asked everone we knowed to kindly let us rest when we was at home. If they wanted a sneak at the babies, they could go bother the hospital and peer at them through the window of the nursery. Everbody had been real kind to leave us in peace.

When I heard the doorbell ring, I saw that Uncle Wind had ignored not us, but our request. When I opened the door, Uncle Wend's eyes got big as he took a gander at me. "Boy, you look like the ass end of bad luck!" I knowed I must truly look dreadful if Uncle Wend couldn't find five dollar words to describe me.

"Well, I feel like I been drug through a knot hole."

 Then he lifted his head and sniffed. "What in tarnation is that odiferous smell?"

"That, Uncle Wend, is the fragrance we call, *'Attempt to potty train Monte'*. I think I sounded pretty smug.

Hearin his name, Monte come runnin in the livin room, a suspicious lookin wad makin his drawers droop. Hollerin, "Unka Wen!" He grabbed Uncle Wend by the leg like a vise, beamin up at him. "I use big boy pannies now!"

Uncle Wend looked alarmed, at both the smell and at the thought of my son wearin girl's underwear. "Does this child have on *pannies*?" He asked, alarmed, as he tried to peel

Monte's fingers from his leg.

Sighin, I said, "No. But in this house at this point in time, I'd be satisfied if he had on combat boots and a chiffon evenin gown. At least he wouldn't be runnin around nekkid."

I pried him off Uncle Wend and took him to the bathroom, lockin the door, so Monte couldn't escape in mid-clean up, bare bottomed. I heard Uncle Wend begin to blather on about somethin to Bensy.

When we come out, he was holdin aloft his gift he had brought for the quads.

"They's called a Whimmy-diddle," He explained, as he showed Bensy the tiny little wooden marionette lookin dolls. "I made one for each of them, and of course, one of each for your other offspring, too."

I opened my mouth to ask him when he thought they'd be old enough to play with them before demolishin them with one crash, one fire, one fall, or who knows what else.

He held up his hand: "I know this isn't an appropriate gift for their ages. This is somethin y'all can store and give them when they are old enough to take care and not damage them." He gave a scrunched up nose look at Monte. "When this tatterdemalion can act like a civilized man, he can play with this precious toy."

Monte grinned. "I tattermalen!"

"You probably are," I muttered and scooped him up. "We thank you, Uncle Wend. We'll be sure and put the whinydiddles-"

"Whimmy-diddles! Good lord, man, has havin offspring addled your brain till nothin comes out but godwottery?"

"I'm sure it has." I looked around for his hat, found it atop Monte's applesauced head, handed it to Uncle Wend, and ushered him to the front door before he said some other big word I didn't understand. "Thanks for droppin by. Come back when the babies come home."

I closed the door behind him. "When they's about twenty," I muttered.

We barely had time to get our heads back on straight when the doorbell rung again.

We was expectin this one, though.

It was obvious to us already that they wadn't no way we could take care of all these babies, no matter how committed our friends and family was. After all, they had lives, too, and we figured in about a month or so after all the babies was home, people would get mighty tired of stayin at our house, no matter what they said they'd do.

A woman had called us, sayin she was the mother of three; ages three, four and five (Lord help her). Since her youngest was startin preschool, she wondered if we'd need any help. She could help two mornins a week and ever other Saturday for five hours. She wanted three dollars a hour.

This seemed crazy. But she went on to explain that she hated to even take that much, but figured that'd pay for her gas. She just wanted to be around babies. She had references out the wazoo, plus my mama knowed her mama.

She and her husband was comin to talk to us today.

I was thankful Uncle Wend had got gone before he could dazzle them with his silver tongue act.

We opened the door to Wincy and Ham Hamilton. Wincy was the one what was goin to help babysit; Ham was her husband.

After proper introductions and offerin them a seat, Bensy offered them somethin to drink. To which Wincy replied, "Lord, woman, if anybody here is waitin on anybody here, it won't be you!" Then she giggled. "I think this was meant to be. Our names rhyme!"

And so they did.

We got comfortable, and they showed us pictures of their children with a big fat dog. Its face looked like a Redbone Coonhound, but it had to be a mix of some sort, cause Redbone's don't get fat.

We bragged on what fine lookin children they had, then I asked, "Ham, what kinda dog you got there? Sure looks well fed!"

"Oh, that picture was took the day we got Lucy back from her bein kidnapped and all." He said this rather calmly and it took me a minute to run through their children's names to make sure he wadn't talkin about younguns gettin kidnapped. That left the dog.

"Somebody kidnapped your dog?"

Ham nodded his head. "Shore did. Lucy is a registered Redbone Coonhound. One of the finest lines you'll find. I'd had her out huntin with my Bluetick Coonhound, equally a fine, fine dog. They took off, a'treein something. I waited, and eventually John Boy, that's the Bluetick, he come back. But Lucy never did." He shook his head sadly. "We kept a'waitin, thankin she'd show back up in a day or two, but she never did. I took her for dead or stole. About a month later, my phone rung and it was a man by the name of Smithers. Said he thought he had my dog. Now, I'm a'thinkin, if this feller's got Lucy, and she's been gone a month, either she's escaped from sommers else or he's gonner be astin for money. But he went on to say he'd had her three weeks, but didn't know it until that day."

"How in the thunder could that be so?" I interrupted. "Did he have a pen full and just happen to count 'em up?"

Ham laughed. "Well, I's right suspicious, that's the truth. Then he explained his five year old little girl had been out to her play house in the back of their yard and Lucy had come up to her, hungry as could be. His little girl fed the dog, locked her in the play house and kept her there. She walked her twice a day if she thought nobody was a'lookin and snuck and fed her Twinkies and doughnuts and cake and the like. Mr. Smither's happened to see her on that particular day walkin this fatter'n-a-hog dog, and went out to see where it'd come from. The little girl told him the story, endin with, can I keep him, please, but of course the man saw the collar, which by now was so tight it was near chokin Lucy to death, on account'a she'd got so fat. Mr. Smithers went through the whole story of how a family was missin the dog. So his girl understood the owners had to come fetch her. You kin imagine my surprise when I pull up and see my fine dog lookin like she'd swallered a watermelon whole." He laughed. "Durn dog still won't come to nuthin but the name Cookie. Won't come to Lucy no more a'tall." We all laughed. "Her daddy went and bought her a Whippet and said if she could fatten it up, he wanted to see it happen."

The deal was struck, Wincy beamin like she'd won the lottery. "I'll be junin around this house afore you know it. With all them litt'luns comin home, this whole joint will be jumpin!"

As they started to leave, Ham said, "Don't take no wooden nickels, now." We learned that's what he always said, instead of good-bye.

CHAPTER ELEVEN

Well, the big day arrived. Bensy kissed me good-bye; all the jokin gone out of her. "Are you sure this is safe and all?" She looked in my eyes.

I'd researched it, and talked to a friend who'd had a vasectomy. For the most part, the information was fairly comfortin, at least as comfortin as you can feel; since you *really* feel you are goin to your doom. Ever time I started readin about somethin bad that had happened, I skipped it. I didn't want to know.

"I don't reckon it can be near as bad as what you just went through, and you're a standin here, ain't you?"

"Barely." Ron beeped the horn. He'd done been to the door, but I guess when he got in the car and I didn't follow, he was urgin me on.

"I gotta go. Ron will be late for work if I don't get a move on."

"And you're okay with Mabel bringin you home?"

"Not really, but she offered to do it. She says I'll be done just in time for lunch. She'll drop me off here and go on her merry way. I think it'll do her heart good to see my sufferin."

Bensy laughed. "You're probably right, honey." She reached and kissed my cheek. "I've got whitey tightys ready. And a ice pack. And the kids won't come near you for a week, if I have to kill 'em."

"Don't do that. The supply and demand will have shifted."

I squeezed her hand and ran down the steps to my doom.

They gave me somethin to calm me down when I got there, because my blood pressure and pulse rate was up. Dr. Cutts joked about it until I reminded him if I died he got custody of the quadruplet newborns, and if Bensy got a sympathetic jury, would have to put all six of my children through college.

The surgery wadn't all that bad, in fact the ride home with Mabel was far worse. She assured me the pain would increase soon, and she was right.

I hobbled in, swallered four ibuprofen, took to our bed with a icepack and slept for three hours.

Let's just say havin two people unable to walk upright in the same household isn't pretty. Bensy's mama saw it was hopeless and took the younguns home with her, while my mama stayed and fed us.

But time goes by, things get better, and in a few days we was both feelin on the mend.

Oh, I got lots of kiddin. My boss called and said he knowed I couldn't do hard labor for a few days, but Jeanne, the secretary, had called in sick and could I answer the phone?

After all, now that I'd been "fixed" people probably couldn't tell my voice from hers no how.

I hung up on him as he was laughin hisself silly at his own joke.

I figured nobody needed a job that bad. If I got fired for hangin up, I felt sure the unemployment office would understand my side.

Things went pretty smooth until Lilly Anne got home from preschool excited to see us both. She hugged Bensy for all she was worth. Before I could remember to stop her; she grabbed me, bangin her head right into my crotch. I screamed like a girl, grabbed aholt of myself and moaned.

Lilly Anne began to wail. "Oh, Da, I sorry! It was oopsadential-like! I didn't mean to!" She put her face in her hands. Wracked with sobs, she fell to her knees, and I felt lower than a snake's belly in a wagon rut.

I eased myself down in the chair and closed my eyes for a second. "Lilly Anne, get in my lap. Careful like, just climb up and set on my leg."

"For sure?"

"Come on." She very carefully did so, and laid her wet face against my shirt. "Miz Wincy said your Mr. Wiggles had a boo-boo and I should be ever so careful, and I wadn't." She sniffed loudly.

"Mr. Wiggles?"

"Yeah, Daddy, you know. Mason has one. It's where you go pee."

"Er, yes, I know. Anyway, you didn't mean to. It's all right now."

"You sure?" She looked up at me, her beautiful eyelashes webbed with tears.

"Yes, honey. Now go on and play. It won't be long before supper."

She scampered off, relieved to be gone, I reckon. Myself? I couldn't wait to get to the bathroom and see if I was bleedin to death or somethin tragic had happened to Mr. Wiggles.

****

Bensy and me wadn't feelin good enough for church on Sunday, so Mama said she'd come by for Lilly Anne if I had her ready to go. She said Monte wadn't worth foolin with yet.

I thought Lilly Anne looked right cute. Between Bensy and me, she'd got a bath and her hair washed. Bensy laid out her clothes and I got oatmeal and toast down her, washed her face and hands and brushed her teeth, and got her dressed.

Mama come flyin in, hollered hey to Bensy and took a long look at Lilly Ann.

"Don't you like her dress?" I asked, for she was starin at it.

"I like it just fine. I'd like it better if it wadn't on backerds."

I peered closely. "How can you tell the diff'rence?"

Mama's mouth twitched, tryin to hold in laughter. "Well, let's see. Dresses are generally zipped up the back, not the front. The bow is tied in the back, not the front. The collar parts in the back, not the front. And the tag goes in the back."

"Daaadeeee." Lilly Anne looked at me accusinly.

"I'm sorry! I didn't know. We'll fix it."

Mama reached over, untied, unzipped and had her out and in it in a jiffy, and they was off.

I ain't figured out if Lilly Anne will forgive me or not.

When Mama brought Lilly Anne home, she mentioned Granny was sick. "I don't think it's serious. She won't go to the doctor. Do you mind checkin on her in the mornin? I got to go to a doctor appointment myself."

I told her so did I, but I'd check on Granny on my way home, if she thought that was soon enough. She said she did, as she allowed her and Daddy was goin to spend most Sunday afternoon with her.

Gettin outta bed the next day was easier than it had been at. I was relieved that I was healin good. I cleaned up after I got the kids fed, and then Bensy and me sat and ate a good breakfast while the kids watched "Veggie Tales".

Dr. Cutts give me a clean bill of health, tellin me to take it easy for a few more weeks. Unless I had a problem I didn't need to see him again, except for the tests to determine that I was sperm free, so to speak.

He didn't have to tell me twice. I threatened to kiss Mabel good-bye; she threatened to have me arrested. It was a happy endin for all.

When I got to Granny's, I hollered through the screen, and she hollered back to come on in.

"Come in if you can stand it. I ain't had a bath in two days, fer I ain't felt like it."

"Well, Granny, if you missed your Saturday bath, it may be too hard on a feller's nose."

She cackled. "Used to that family that lived up the road – Dester and 'em - you know who I'm talkin about?"

"Cain't say as I do."

"Oh, yes, you do! Her mama was a Sellers from down Savannah way."

"Oh."

"Anyways, they never took a bath on Saturday night, nor no other un, either." She shook her head. "Shore didn't want to visit them none in the summer time."

"I reckon not."

She went on about five more minutes about "Dester and 'em", while I sat patiently noddin my head, wise enough now to pretend I knowed exactly who she was talkin about, even if they'd been dead twenty-five years before I was even thought about.

After takin a deep breath from all that, she asked, "So how you a'doin after bein cut and all?"

"I ain't been *cut*, Granny. Not like a hog. And I'm doin just fine. In fact, I come from the doctor right before I got here. He released me. I still cain't lift nothin heavy for a week or so, but I'm healin right nice." I dared not mention goin back to be tested, for I feared she'd ask how that was accomplished.

She snickered. "Orta make Bensy happy, anyhow. That is ifen she ever recovers from poppin out four younguns. Lord, I don't know how she stood it hardly."

"Well, it happened awful fast. And they was little, if that makes any difference."

She nodded her head. "How's them babies comin along?"

"They's doin good. The doctors said we might be able to bring Luke and John Mark home in about ten days. They's all gainin weight. But those two was the biggest to begin with, and are over four pounds. If they keep that up, they'll come home soon. They are all healthy, though."

"Praise the Lord," Granny said. "And is that devil Monte potty trained yet?"

"Er, no. But we are workin on it. He's doin better, especially durin the day."

Somebody knocked on the door. I glanced out the window. "It's Uncle Wend."

Granny said a word she ought not to.

"Go ahead. Let the fool in. Just give me a minute to turn down my hearin aids."

I rolled my eyes and went to the door.

"Well, hello there, Charlie!"

I hate bein called – well, you know.

"Got the collywobbles yet?" he asked, slappin me on the back.

Before I could answer, which would have been, '*Heck if I know*', Granny walked to the door. "Hello there, Wend."

"Hello, Lemma! I heard you was feelin a bit under the weather and I come to see if I could be of assistance."

"I'm a mite better now. How's Marveena gettin along?"

"She is indubitably grand. Since we have started

perambulatin about the neighborhood early each mornin, we are in much better spirits throughout the day. Of course, we each do pandiculation first." He smiled like a big old possum.

"Don't everbody?" Granny asked.

I coughed into my hand, excused myself and headed for the bathroom.

Lord!

I counted to a hundred, hopin he'd be gone, but no, he had made hisself comfortable while Granny served him coffee and some rather dry lookin pound cake.

"Granny, you been sick. You don't need to be up *servin* folks," I said, givin Uncle Wend a meaninful look.

He flapped a hand at me. "I tried to convince her otherwise, but bein a lady of good upbringin, she wouldn't say no."

I bet.

He propped his saucer of cake on his belly and slurped his coffee. "Ah, simply delicious. Thank you, Lemma. But I must run." He heaved hisself off the couch, shakin his head as he shook the crumbs off his belly onto the floor. I made a note to myself to sweep up before I left. "I have to be meetin with that snollygoster, Councilman Foster. He's accusin me of tryin to sway folks about the vote for fluoride in the city water. Why, why would I even care? I don't live within the city limits."

"No, I cain't imagine you carin about anythang that didn't directly involve you." Granny said.

"Certainly not! It's pure godwottery!"

"I'm sure." I stood up with him. "Well, let me see you to the door. I need to clean up in here before I leave."

That sailed right over his big, inflated head.

He left, I swept up, saw that Granny had laid back down and made her promise she'd go to the doctor if she wadn't completely well tomorrow.

She called the next day and said she reckoned she better go on to the doctor, she wadn't feelin much better and started thinkin on missin stuff with the babies if she didn't get well quick.

So off we went to see Doc Maddlyn early the next mornin. When we walked in the waitin room Granny pointed toward the sign in sheet, and handed me her big old pocket book. Not exactly a manly look, but I was used to it. I signed her in, gave the girl the insurance papers she needed, and she handed me a clipboard with a bunch of foolishness to fill out. Then I went to set myself down.

Granny was already engaged in a lively conversation with the woman settin next to her, and she barely acknowledged my presence.

Of course, she informed me *she* wadn't gonna fill out all that nonsense, and for me to do the best I could with it.

Ever time I had to interrupt her conversation to ask a question, she got more and more annoyed.

But one had me completely stumped. "I hate to interrupt again," I said sarcastically, "but they's askin if there is a illness or a condition that seems to show up frequently in your family."

"Well, we all complain a awful lot."

"So, how do you spell hypochondria?" I asked the nurse. Several people in the waitin room snickered, but I figured truth's truth.

Turned out Granny was a little anemic and had a sinus infection, too. They give her some vitamins to take and some medicine for the infection and told her if she wadn't better in five days to call and come back in.

She got better, and was soon as bossy as ever.

CHAPTER TWELVE

Time went by. I got completely healed up, Bensy got all well, Monte used the potty durin the day, and we was goin to pick up Luke and John Mark first thing the next mornin.

This seemed like a dream. After two months of livin on the road – to the hospital, to work, to here, to there – it didn't seem possible we was actually bringin babies home.

The doctor had talked to us at length about bringin two babies home at one time. "These babies have never been separated. We feel like some of them need to be together all the time. Luke and John Mark are your biggest babies, and although nothin is really wrong with any of the quads, we'd like to get the other two a little heavier before lettin them go home. Maybe another week." He smiled. "Plus, this will ease you into havin multiple babies to take care of."

Right.

Bensy had been adamant from the beginnin that the babies be in one big "bed" so they could touch and sense each other's presence. Of course, the medical staff balked; they'd wanted them each in a separate container. But the hospital's nursery social worker had sided with Bensy. Reluctantly, the staff had agreed to give it a try, and now believed the babies was healthier than they would have otherwise been.

Go Bensy!

The boys we was bringin home each weighed right at five

pounds, which was hefty considerin how they had started out. I reckon five pounds was a magic number for all these little fellers.

****

I contacted Mr. Parker and told him two of my boys was comin home, in case he wanted to do some photo shots with the van. But he declined. Said we'd arrange a professional photographer to come to the hospital the day the last baby was released and could 're-enact' the scene as if they was all bein loaded for the first time, which was fine by me.

Now, it's one thing to hold and rock tiny newborns while you are surrounded by hospital staff. It's altogether different when you are strappin 'em down in a vehicle about to hurdle down the highway and take them home with no medical staff in sight. To say I was scared spitless is a great understatement.

Monte and Lilly Ann was beside theirselves when we walked in the door, a baby in each of our arms. Lilly Ann was clappin her hands, squealin till one of the grannies shushed her. We set down on the couch and let them come over and talk and touch.

Bensy and me decided that we'd take turns with feedins, that way we'd get a few chunks of solid hours of sleep. Ha.

After a week, Monte had reverted back to pull-ups; I reckon the stress was too much for him.

And after ten days, the hospital said we could bring home Paula and Matthew the followin Wednesday, which gave us two more days of only havin two babies at home.

It was a big to-do, as the Parker twins was on alert and had the van at the hospital. Bensy's mama was gonna drive our old wagon back home so we could all pose for the van pictures and load up the babies.

Bensy had Lilly Ann and Monte all spiffy and cute, and they'd been threatened with their very lives if they even got one hair out of place.

Zeke Parker had nice lookin metallic advertisements on each side of the van. I reckon if you have to drive around like you are in a billboard, it might as well be in good taste.

If that's even possible.

I guess I'm just plain dumb. But I did not expect newspaper reporters and the local TV and radio people to be there when we exited the hospital. I had Paula, Bensy had John Mark, Mama had Matthew and Bensy's mama had Luke. My granny had Lilly Ann by the hand and Bensy's granny had Monte. They was a big family portrait, and it made me feel right bad for our daddies what wadn't there, but was holdin down the fort at home.

They interviewed Bensy, and I was right proud of her. She looked handsome and talked like she'd been in front of cameras all her life.

Me, on the other hand, grinned like a goon and stuttered like a half-wit. Not bad, for me.

The van drove like a dream. Let's just say I ain't never had a new car before. It smelled new, it drove new....and I dreaded usin it, because its days was numbered to look like a beauty queen.

I just thought we'd been stressed out.

Do you have *any* idey how utterly chaotic it is to have a three year old, a two year old who has backslid in the potty trainin department and four tiny babies under your care?

No, you do not. Don't even try to pretend you do.

The good Lord only knows what we would have done without our mamas and the two grannies. The church and Bible study groups and the quiltin society brought food and babysat Monte and Lilly Ann and was our gofers, too.

But exhaustion filled ever inch of our bodies, plumb down through our bones.

Company was expected, but not exactly welcomed, if you know what I mean.

Still, folks felt like they had to drop by, certainly those we was especially close to.

Ron come by late one mornin on his way to do a half shift, as someone had gone home sick and they promised him double pay.

After the preliminary howdies, he said he'd come by to see Bensy and me, and to cheer us up. So he proceeded to share what he'd found.

"I found this here birth announcement in a 1911 newspaper." He commenced to read: *'Mr. Tim Dover of near this place is the proud parent of Triplets; three fine boy babies who arrived Sunday night. He and the Mrs. have had three sets of twins before this besides seven others so that now they have in all sixteen children, all livin and healthy. We congratulate the Dovers on their good fortune. This is a great country for raisin babies anyway.'* He looked up and beamed, handin the clippin to Bensy.

She read it again, then looked up at Ron. "What was the mother's name?"

"Huh?"

"The mother." Bensy said impatiently. "Her name ain't even mentioned. *She's* the one who had all them babies. Why ain't her name mentioned in the piece?"

Oh, lord. I could see Bensy's color risin in her face. She was beginnin to look somewhat like a beet.

"I don't reckon they did it that way back then," Ron stammered.

"Well, they should have! You men want to take all the credit for what happens, when it's the woman's body what produces more than enough for one child. And who do you think carried them babies and delivered them babies?"

Oh, lord, again.

"That poor woman! Do you think she had help from that man washin all them diapers, feedin all them babies? It was 1911 for goodness sakes!" Bensy was standin up now, and Ron was backin up. "This is outlandish! This is – is – *sinful*! That's what it is! You take this paper and show it to your wife. Ask her what she thinks about this piece of sh-"

"Bensy!" I hollered and looked down at Lilly Ann and Monte, who had been watchin a DVD, but was now starin slack mouthed at their mama.

She slumped, grabbed a tissue and tore outta the room.

"Thanks for comin by, Ron." I said. "It's been a real pleasure."

Ron sat down and sighed. "I thought this was such a good idey. How was I to know she wouldn't like it?"

"Your own wife had twins and is carryin another child. Do you believe Mara would think it was cute that the woman ain't give no credit in a *birth announcement*?" I realized my voice was gettin higher and I was sorta soundin like Bensy. I cleared my throat. "Look, we'll laugh at this in a year – or two – but for now you better take this back home with you." I nodded toward the piece of paper. "Keep it in a safe place, away from Mara. After all the new babies start school, bring it back out."

Ron shook his head. "I ain't even got to hold a single baby, and yore kickin me out."

I sighed and glanced at our bedroom door. "Come on," I said in a very soft voice. "I'll take you to them. But if they ain't awake, you don't hold nobody." Then I glared at Lilly Ann and Monte. "Follow me," I threatened them, "and no DVDs for the rest of the day."

The nursery had four baby beds, but the quads was all in one. They was laid side by side, sideways in the one bed. They reminded me of a pile of puppies or kittens. They was all asleep, crammed next to each other. Even though they was still little bitty, they had managed to move enough to get right on top of each other, nearly.

"Glory be," Ron whispered, his eyes widenin. "Look at that. Did you find out if any of 'em is identical?"

"Yeah. The boys are identical triplets. Paula just come along for the ride."

"Well, they all look alike to me. Can you tell 'em apart?"

"I usually know which one is Paula when I do a diaper change."

Ron chuckled. Then he shook his head. "You better be glad you got fixed, or Bensy would never let you touch her again."

"I feel like a yard dog. Granny talked about me gettin cut,

now you are sayin I was fixed."

"Oh, I ain't pokin fun. It's just hard to say – that word – because as soon as Mara and this baby is fine after the birth, I'll be a member of the club. We figger three is enough."

"I thought one was enough."

Ron barked out laughter and Matthew – or maybe it was Luke – or maybe it was – anyway, a baby jumped. We left the nursery quietly.

Bensy was comin out of our bedroom at the same time. She looked a right smart better than when she went runnin in. She held her arms out to Ron and they hugged. "I'm sorry for bein so emotional, Ron. Will you forgive me?"

"Lord, Bensy, you need to forgive me. I never thought about upsettin you. Wouldn't do it for the world."

"I know. Let's call it even and forget about it, all right?"

"Fine with me."

Ron said this at the same time Monte started yellin, "I got to poop!" which woke up some of the babies, who started mewlin.

Ron looked at his watch, said, "I gotta go!" and did.

CHAPTER THIRTEEN

As the babies got a little bit bigger, and Wincy became a routine fixture at the house, I decided we needed a barn cat. I mean, what's a barn without a cat?

I heard the neighbor down the road had a cat with a new litter that was almost ready to give away, so I called her up. All I said was I was interested in a kitten, and she told me to come on over.

Boy, was I in for a surprise.

My neighbor was Miz Tandy Burton, and she invited me right in. "I have two kittens, actually, if you are interested."

She led me into her livin room, and I swan, there sat the biggest cat I have ever laid eyes on outside the bobcat I saw one night diggin in our garbage.

"This is Precious." She laughed. "My granddaughter, who was three at the time, named her. Of course, that's not the name on her papers."

"What kind of cat is that?" I asked. "Part mountain lion?"

"Well, they say part lynx and Angora, a long time ago. She's a Maine Coon."

She was beautiful. Her long silky hair was almost silver, not quite white.

"I'm afraid we had a bit of an accident, and she got pregnant with the neighbor-down-the-road-tomcat. I had no idea she was even comin into season, but I should have known when she ran out the door. She'd never done anything like that, bein a housecat and all. But old Mr. Tom was waitin right outside and they rendezvoused right off the bat."

She did a come here motion with her finger and pointed behind the couch. Piled on top of one another, sound asleep, was three kittens. One looked just like the mama, one was a red tabby and one was black with some white on it.

"They are all three boys. I'm keepin the silver tip. The tom is a big cat – probably twelve or thirteen pounds. Precious weighs around eighteen pounds, so I figure these boys will be pretty hefty. I obviously cain't sell them, but I do want to know they'll have good homes."

I squirmed a little, but felt like I had to tell her the truth, and was thankin the good Lord I hadn't asked Lilly Ann to come with me like I'd thought about doin. 'Cause I figgered Miz Burton wadn't gonna let me have one of these for a barn cat.

"Well, I can tell you it'd be treated fine. But I have to be honest. I wanted me a cat for the barn."

She eyed me. "I tell you what. Take both of them. If they aren't goin to be housecats, they'll need each other. And promise me you'll keep them in the house until they are three months old. At two months, they just aren't ready to be out when they've never known anything but this." She motioned around her house.

"Are you sure?"

"Oh, I'll be checkin on you, at least for a time or two. I don't trust my darlins to just anyone. But Maine Coons are known to be great mousers, and if they have shelter and food and water and some affection, they'll do fine."

She walked over and picked the red one up. He looked at her sleepily. "This one looks just like his daddy, cuss him. Red tabbies can be pretty big, just on their own, so he ought to be a big one. He has a Latin name: Red, for red." She laughed. She put him back down and picked up the black and white one. "This is Panda. He is what is called a tuxedo, because of his black and white markins." She held up his feet, which was huge and looked like baseball mitts. "His grandmother on the Maine Coon side was a polydactyl, six claws on the front, five on the back. She was also a tuxedo, and he looks just like her. So he may be a monster, too."

I reached for him before I even knowed what I was doin. She handed him to me, and he snuggled right under my chin.

This didn't look good at all.

I sighed. "Okay. We can put a litter box on the screen porch out next to the kitchen, and make a pet door. I cain't have it inside because Monte – that's my two-year-old – would be in it with his toy cars. You cain't trust that boy no further than you can throw him. That way they can be house cats for a month."

She smiled, got a cat carrier for me to take them in, sayin I could return it any time, shook my hand and off I went.

Somethin bothered me, though. She had the nastiest little twinkle in her eye, as though she knowed somethin I didn't.

She did.

When I got home, the kids went crazy over them, and Bensy did, too. We had an old plastic storage box I used for a litter box, which I filled with clean sand until I could get to the store for litter later on that day.

We had a couple of cans of cat food left over from Granny's old yard cat that had died a year ago. With that and a bowl of fresh water, they was all set.

We did the 'be gentle with them' speech, and let Lilly Ann and Monte hold them. Monte learned he wadn't quite gentle enough and got a bite on the nose. It was only a nip, but he left the kittens alone for the rest of the day, and never rough housed with them again. Lilly Ann took turns with them, carryin them round like they was babies, which they liked just fine.

That night, when I went to check on the kids before my bedtime, there was a kitten curled up in each of their beds. Bensy took pictures.

And that's when I figured out the twinkle in Tandy Burton's eyes. She knowed exactly what she was up to. Keep them in the house a month, I still wouldn't have a barn cat, I'd have housecats.

But that was all right, I reckon.

CHAPTER FOURTEEN

Bensy and me had been up almost all night. Lilly Ann and Monte was both sick, and I was tendin them, tryin to keep them away from the babies, and she was stuck with them four.

I was beyond tuckered. All the younguns was asleep, as was Bensy.

I had just got set down and rared back in the recliner when the phone rung.

I wouldn't have had it any other way.

It was Ron Summers. He apologized for callin, but I told him I was happy to talk to him any day of the week.

"I just had to tell somebody what happened a few minutes ago, and you was the first to come to mind."

He sounded right excited, but there was somethin else in his tone, maybe amusement.

"Lay it on me."

"You remember Dolly's bull calf, right?"

"Ron, if I live to be a hunderd, I won't forget Dolly's bull calf."

"Yeah, yeah. Anyway, I got a call from the sheriff about two hours ago askin me if I had any livestock missin. I told him I didn't know, I had just walked in the door from work. Mara and the boys had been at her mama's and wadn't home yet. Only thing on my mind was the supper she was bringin home from her mama's. I asked the sheriff did he want to hold on or me call him back, and he said he'd hold on, this was important. It made sense to me right then they had some stolen cattle on their hands and was tryin to figger whose it was."

"Sounds like it to me. Was it yours?"

"Shore was. I went to the barn, and wouldn't you know it, poor old Dolly's bull calf was missin again. She looked at me pitiful like and mooed at me. I petted her and told her I was doin the best I could. So, I went back to the house and confirmed with the sheriff I had a bull calf missin. He said, *'I knowed it! I knowed it was yours. He's a fine lookin animal, I tell you that.'* 'You mean you got him?' I asked him. *'Right here. He's in one of the cells, fer I didn't have no place else to put him. Tell me his markins and stuff so we can make it official and you can come and bail him out.'*

"The sheriff thought he was real funny, I reckon. I wrote a note to Mara to tell her where I was, and went back to town."

"Who stole him?"

"You know the Bronsons that moved here six months or so ago? Had two full grown boys with them?"

"Vaguely."

"Well, them boys stay in trouble, and don't work any better'n antenna reception. You ain't gonna believe this story. One of the deputies was settin up on Dusty Road to do a little radar work before dark when this bright red sedan drove by, goin real slow. The deputy said he wouldn't even paid no attention to the car, except it was goin so slow. As he watched it mosey on by, he said he coulda swore he saw the silhouette of a cow in the back seat. Well, that didn't sit right with him, so he hopped in the patrol car and caught up with them which wadn't hard, since they was creepin along. He blue lighted them, and they pulled over, real slow like. The deputy got outta his car and walked over to the driver's side. 'Howdy,' he said and the Broson boy drivin howdied in return like there wadn't nothin unusual about a calf ridin around in his backseat. 'Mind me askin what you're a'doin with that bull calf in your car?' the deputy asked. They allowed that was a reasonable question and said they'd purchased it on the spur of the moment for a friend who'd been lookin for just that very thing for his pa a present. Have you ever heard such durn foolishness in your life?" Ron asked.

"Cain't say as I have. But that ain't illegal in and of itself, is it?"

"Don't know. Deputy said he explained to them it looked a wee bit suspicious and would like to see a bill of sales, which of course they could not produce. The calf commenced to carry on – they had it strapped in the seat with a seat belt – and the deputy told him he thought that calf was needin its mama for supper. I don't reckon them boys knowed what to say to that.

"Anyway, he convinced them to follow him to the sheriff's department. He looked at the tag in the calf's ear and was pretty sure he recognized the info as mine. I still hand tag mine, you know. Sheriff said it took him and the deputy both to get the calf outta the car. They had him in one cell and the Bronson boys in the other one. Creek saw me and started bellerin at me, which made everbody laugh, includin the Bronsons."

"You named that calf Creek?"

"Shore did. After what he put me through, havin to cross that creek and all, he deserved the name. Bettern Wet Britches for a name, I reckon."

I laughed. "I reckon so."

"Them boys are now in jail for cattle rustlin."

"You pressin charges?"

"You bet I am. Creek is worth a lot of money. Plus, his poor mama didn't need no more stress about him disappearin."

For Ron, it always comes down to what makes Dolly happy.

I just hope he treats Mara half as good.

CHAPTER FIFTEEN

Since we was still not quite able to get back to church as a family, and the best we'd been able to do is one of us take Lilly Ann and Monte to Sunday School and dash right back home, I decided I was goin to get back involved in the Brotherhood. Those men of the church was committed to helpin folks in our community what couldn't help theirself. We met once a month, and we did some mighty good stuff for the community.

This month, they was sendin us out two by two to scout the town to see if we could root out some of the families most in need.

I was paired with Sal Hollinsworth, a fella four or five years younger than me. He was datin Tinsie Postell, and everbody figured it was just a matter of time before weddin bells chimed.

Talkin about nothin, we cruised through one of the poorest neighborhoods in town.

"Old Marvin Butts could sure use a helpin hand. He's got nearly as many younguns as I do and he got laid off three months ago at the mill. I don't hardly seen how they's gettin by."

Sal snorted. "We knowed they needed help real bad. I told the Brotherhood I'd deliver." He said. "So, the Brotherhood got some stuff for the kids and some food – you know –

canned goods, bread, stuff like that, to try and help them out. Instead, they helped me out."

"How's that?" I asked, my interest growin.

"Marvin helped me right off his property with a double barreled shotgun. Didn't want no charity, accordin to him. Rather let his younguns go hungry. And they are."

I shook my head. "As far as I'm concerned, that's child abuse. Them kids cain't help who they are or where they are, and their daddy orght to be shot, or at least humble his foolish pride, and let them kids have food. If he thinks hunger is better than charity, he don't have to eat the stuff."

Sal looked at me in a rather peculiar way. "Can I talk to you sometime?"

"Sure." That got up curiosity. "You got time after this?"

"Yeah."

He was pretty quiet after that until we saw Hoss Smith out in his yard with his bulldog. The dog (and Hoss, too, for that matter) was as big as a house. The dog was solid white. Name was Rhino.

I opined how I'd love me a bulldog, too.

Sal grinned. "Now I can help you with that. My nephew, Sammy, has a bulldog he's got to give to a good home because he's goin off to school. It's about to kill him, too. I figure if I can help that dog be happy, Sammy will be happy."

I shrugged. "Won't hurt for him to stop by sometime. I ain't promisin nothin, though."

"Sounds fair."

"Does the dog like cats?"

"I don't know. You got a cat?"

"Two good sized kittens. They own the place."

Sal laughed. "When Sammy gets hold of you, you can ask him."

We got to my house after the meetin. All younguns was in the bed asleep. Of course, Sal had to see the babies. He was real quiet and awestruck.

Bensy excused herself and said she was goin to lay down while she could, the babies would be up in a few hours, hungry.

We sat and Sal squirmed in the chair a little. "Most people don't know much about me."

"You mean cause of movin down here when you was little?"

"Well, yeah, but also because Mama and Papa never talked. Thank God."

I raised my eyebrows at that. "What do you mean, Sal?"

"Mama and Papa adopted me when I was nearly eight years

old. I'd been placed in foster care in New York, where I was born, and where my mother was raisin me – if you can call it that – after my father disappeared. I think he was tired of a crazy wife."

"I didn't know you was adopted. I just thought your parents lived up North for a while, had you, and moved back."

"They asked me what I wanted folks to know. I told them I didn't want folks to know anything. So that's why they kept their mouths shut."

"Well, l did wonder why two southerners would name their kid Sal."

He laughed. "It's short for Salvatore. My father's family was Italian. And you're right. Nobody from down here in their right mind would use that name. Mama and Papa made up some stuff about namin me after a great-great-grandparent, or somethin. I told them I'd change my name, but they said no. That was part of who I was."

"Makes sense, I guess. It'd be hard to be called Billy Bob after Sal for eight years."

"I hear ya." He shook his head.

Actually, I was sittin there tryin to figure out why he was tellin me this; heck, why he was even here. Sal was several years younger, and although we was in the same Sunday School class, it wadn't like we'd hung out before.

Sal huffed out a breath. "Look, I need to tell somebody and get some advice other than my parents. They think I can do no wrong."

I grinned. "Can we swap parents?"

He chuckled. "I am doted on, still, and me a grown man. Anyhow, I think I have found someone. I love her, and I believe she loves me-"

"You mean Tinsie?"

He looked shocked. "How'd you know that?"

"Everbody has knowed for some time, except you, apparently." I grinned at him. "Ever time you look at her you get all dopey eyed."

"Well, crap!" He shook his head in disbelief. "Does anybody know when I'm gonna ask her to marry me?"

"Naw. We was wonderin, though."

Sal shook his head. "I want to right away. But she doesn't know my story. No one here did, till you. I want her to know – I want her to know my birth mother was very unstable. I was too little to know if it was a mental illness or drugs, but sometimes I didn't get food, or took to school – stuff like that. Things actually got better for me when I started kindergarten because I got breakfast and lunch every day I was there. Somebody got me a good coat." He closed his eyes for a moment. "In first grade, we was havin a

Halloween party. I went home all excited, askin her to get me a costume. Little kids ain't got much sense sometimes. Why I thought she could do this without screwin up, when she couldn't even feed me over half the time, I'll never know. Well, she got excited about it, too. Dressed me up like a girl."

"Oh, no!" I whispered.

"Yep. Walked me to school, all proud. Of course, all the other boys was cowboys and firemen. The whole class froze when I walked in, even the teacher. And Ma just looked proud, she was so clueless. Everyone thawed out and started laughin like crazy. Of course, the teacher tried to make them behave." He dropped his voice. "They called me Sally the rest of the time I was there."

"That may be the worst story I ever heard." I meant it, too. I could imagine a six-year-old bein tortured like that. "Who stopped them callin you Sally?"

"That's when I was taken from Ma. Not because of the outfit, but because of her appearance and behavior at school that day. I don't remember, but Mama and Papa said Social Services told them she was filthy, barefoot, and had lipstick smeared all over her face. She apparently thought she looked okay. She wasn't coherent, either."

"It musta been awful bein taken away like that."

"Nope. Got put with a nice family in another school district shortly thereafter." He grinned. "Then they adopted me. We moved here at the end of my second grade year."

"I like happy endins. I think you ain't got nothin to worry about tellin Tinsie. She loves you, clear as day."

Sal leaned closer. "But what about havin kids? If Ma was crazy, could my kids inherit that? How do I know?"

"Well, we take a risk havin kids, no matter what our history. But cain't you ask Social Services up there to look in your record and get some information? Maybe a family history?"

"I hadn't thought of that." He was quiet, thinkin. "Scares me to death – like she'll pop outta the pages and grab me." He slapped his knees and stood up. "Good advice. I been prayin about who to talk to, and after tonight, I knew God was leadin me to you. Thank you." He stuck out his hand, and we shook. He promised to keep me updated.

After he left, I just stood there a minute, thinkin. You never know what people are holdin onto inside, do you?

The next mornin, while Bensy was tryin to trick me into tellin her what me and Sal talked about, somebody knocked on the door, right after I said, "I cain't tell you, Bensy. Sal made me swear on a stack of moon pies I wouldn't tell nobody."

I saw it was Sammy, Sal's nephew.

"I brung the dog for you to see."

"Well, okay, I guess. Where is it?"

"In the truck. I'll go get her." He looked like he was about to give me his best friend, and I felt guilty about it.

He opened the cab, and I saw him talkin, and then he hugged the dog. When Sammy brought the dog to the door, she gave two wags of her stumpy tail and sat down, starin at me.

She was a bulldog mix, about 75 or 80 pounds with a black muzzle, white feet and a pale fawn coat that was close to white.

"What kind of mix is this dog?" I asked.

Sammy blushed and looked down at his feet. "Part Boxer."

"And part what else?" He didn't answer. I squatted down so my face was level with the dog's. She looked at me steady, but I could see a slight tremble in her body – anticipation or fear – I couldn't tell.

Since Sammy hadn't answered the question, I asked another. "So how old is she?" I could tell she was a young dog, I figured three to five years old.

He mumbled somethin, that I swan had the word months in it.

I stood up and glared at him, hopin to intimidate him into talkin. "What did you say?"

"She's seven."

"Years?"

"Months."

"Are you tellin me this is a *puppy*?" I almost strangled on the word puppy. An eighty-pound puppy? Good lord!

"Yep. Other part of her is her mama is half Bull Mastiff and half Old English Mastiff. This here dog's daddy was the Boxer."

"What you're tellin me is this dog will be the size of a pony or more by the time she's three years old. That right?"

"Just about."

"You realize I'm havin to feed six children, my wife and myself, not to mention cows and chickens? And you want me to take on a growin horse of a dog?"

"Well-"

About that time, the dog stood up, come to me and leaned into my leg, lookin up at me with clear brown eyes. Then she sat down again – on my foot. Her head rested against my leg. She let out a big sigh, then slid down until her head was restin on my other foot.

"I'll take her. But don't you go braggin to nobody about this, you hear me?"

Sammy grinned. "Yes sir, I reckon I do." He turned to leave, but looked back at me before he jumped into the truck. "Her name is Dancer."

"Why in the world would you name a dog Dancer?"

He grinned again. "You'll see."

Then he got in the truck and drove off. He drove slowly like a little old woman, and I figured that was because he was only fifteen.

I sorta broke all that news to Bensy in pieces. At first, like me, she thought Dancer was a full growed dog, and until she asked me, I didn't offer to tell.

And by then, Dancer had decided she was not my dog. She belonged lock, stock and barrel to Bensy. So it didn't make much difference to Bensy if she got bigger'n a elephant.

Which she did.

I guess I didn't get me a dog after all.

And the Dancer name? Well, evertime one of us went away – even if it was to the barn and back without her – when she saw us again she got up on her hind legs and danced around, tongue hangin out, grinnin to beat the band. Then she'd get on all fours and dance in circles till she wore herself out, at which point she'd come to you and huff and fall on your feet.

At first it was alarmin, then it was cute, then, well, then, you just got used to it.

As far as the cats went, they just assumed the dog was for them to sleep on to keep warm.

CHAPTER SIXTEEN

Granny had graciously agreed to come and help out with the babies while Bensy and me took Lilly Ann and Monte out on the town. It had been a long time, and we felt it was somethin we really needed to do outside the circus of our home. We figured between Wincy, Granny and my mama, the babies would be took real good care of.

I called to see if Granny was ready for me to come get her in the next hour.

"I'm a'just gettin outta the share."

"Oh. I'll call you back in few minutes."

"Naw, I done dried off. I's just standin here greasin up."

Please no mental image, please no – too late. I could picture my old granny greasin up like a pig gettin ready for a race at the county fair.

"Just come on, I'll do jig time and be ready."

So I went on.

****

The first place we headed to with the kids, was the *"Central Confectionary"*. It probably don't need no explanation, but I have to say it was some of the best bakery produce you could ever hope to find. It was run by Dolphus Kincaid and his wife, Kitty. They'd been at it for over thirty years, and one of my greatest fears is they'd retire. They had one boy who was in college, but I didn't figure he'd be reliable to take over the bakery. Then where would we be?

I got me a big old sugar incrusted piece of blackberry pie, Bensy got somethin chocolate and the kids got a cupcake each.

Kitty asked about the babies and her and Bensy talked a while. Dolphus come around the counter and give Lilly Ann a quarter and Monte a little plastic toy soldier.

Then, thanks to my wife bein very smart, we was cleaned up in no time with wet wipes and ready to continue our adventure.

We journeyed to the toy store, where they each got to pick out a toy. Lilly Ann was insistent we buy somethin for the babies, too, so Bensy picked out a set of four cloth baby books that met with Lilly Ann's approval.

As we come out of the toy store, Duff Woodrow's ice cream truck was jinglin down the street.

Havin had no sugar in all of an hour, both younguns commenced to beg for a snow cone.

Given as it was a rare event we was even out here, we agreed.

As you can imagine, I was busy with head and hand; tryin to juggle change and snow cones and not gettin the stuff all over me, while Bensy held onto the kids.

At the worst moment, I hear, "Well, well. We was perambulatin down this way and happened to see part of this lovely family."

I'm sure you'll never guess who that was a'talkin.

I straightened up, handin a snow cone to each youngun as I went. "Hey, Uncle Wend, Aint Marveena."

"Hello, dear boy," Aunt Marveena gushed. She's always liked me a lot. I noticed Bensy rollin her eyes.

"Tell Uncle Wend and Aint Marveena hey, Lilly Ann."

Lilly Ann stuck out her tongue, showin them it was already turnin blue.

"It's the snow cone." I explained. They looked insulted.

"Tell Uncle Wend and Aint Marveena hello, Monte."

He flung hisself around Uncle Wend's leg, as usual, with snow cone in hand, which dripped down Uncle Wend's trouser leg. "Hey, Unca Wend!" he said, a huge grin on his sloppy face.

Uncle Wend prized Monte offa his leg. "My, my, he certainly is an obsequious child." He tried to smile, but I could tell he couldn't hardly stand it.

I really love my kids.

"Where ya'll headed?" I asked.

"Well," Uncle Wend said, "We was headed to the park to stroll among the lovely foliage." He had his hanky out and was tryin to swipe at the snow cone slobber on his pants. "I am tryin to recover from the hebetudinous, cretinous behavior of Brownlow McGhee."

Not that I had a clue what Uncle Wend just said, but I knowed it sounded bad. "What has Brownlow done to you?"

"That cocalorum engaged me in an arglebargle regardin the political office I am considerin."

"Wow." Bensy said. I looked at her and she shrugged.

"Indeed! That snollygoster has dared falsely accuse me! His calumny will not go unnoticed!"

"I bet," I said. In my whole life I'd never heard Uncle Wend go on a verbiage rampage such as this.

"That platitudinous fool will be found out! Only the poor gobemouche will be hornswoggled. He's nothin but a pettifogger!" He shook his fist into the air. "I will not be banjaxed!" And with that, he grabbed Marveena by the arm and marched off. Aint Marveena gave a little wave of her gloved hand, and they was off.

We stood there for a moment, mouths open. "Um, are we still goin to the park?" Bensy asked.

"I ain't sure. Right now I'm feelin a little dizzy."

After we got home, I was tryin to balance the check book when Lilly Ann come runnin up to me. "Daddy, Monte is cawin his banjo a banjax."

"That's because he heard Uncle Wend use that word. It's really a banjo, just like you said."

"Well, den, what does banjax mean?"

Like I knowed.

"I guess we need to look that one up on the computer," I said, gettin outta my chair. "Let's see if we can Google it." I pulled it up. "Banjaxed means to be ruined or broken." I turned to Lilly Ann. "Like if Monte stomped your doll house, it would be banjaxed."

Her lip began to tremble and her eyes filled with big pools of tears. "Or," I said, hurriedly, "you accidentally put your foot through Monte's banjo, it would be banjaxed." She brightened – too much. *"Which you are not goin to do, understand?"* She narrowed her eyes for a moment, but finally nodded in agreement.

She scampered off, and I decided to look up the only other word I remembered in Uncle Wend's tirade. "Pettifogger," as I read the meanin, I started laughin and went to look for Bensy.

She was in the nursery, changin diapers on the assembly line. We had graduated to two baby beds now, as the boys all weighed twelve pounds at age six months. Paula had pulled ahead, weighin thirteen pounds. We had dressed them color coded, green, blue, yellow and pink, because the boys really did look just alike. We had a little ribbon we kept on the boys to be color coded with their clothes. We transferred the ribbon from wrist to ankle to ankle to wrist ever night with their bath, so it wouldn't make a raw place on them.

Bensy handed me John Mark and Matthew so she could diaper Paula. "You remember Uncle Wend callin old Brownlow a pettifogger today?"

"How could I forget?" she shook her head.

"I looked it up. It means 'one who befuddles others with his speech'."

She giggled. "Pot callin kettle black, I reckon." She moved on to the last baby to change. "Why'd you decide to look it up?"

I told her about banjax/banjo. "You better watch Lilly Ann. You've tempted her now."

I sighed heavily. "Don't I know it."

"And speakin of Lilly Ann, take a gander at Paula."

Paula was really comin into her own. The boys had pale blonde hair like down, and bright blue eyes. Paula had curly, reddish brown hair and her eyes was turnin greener ever day. She was beginnin to look more and more like her sister. I wondered if the boys' hair would turn yellower as time went on. Monte's hair was baby duck yellow and stuck straight up, all over his head, no matter how hard Bensy tried to get it to lay down.

"Well, well. Paula isn't gonna have to dress in pink all the time. She has suddenly started lookin totally different." I wiggled my eyebrows at her and she grinned a big old gummy grin at me.

"Let's feed this brood so I can read a little in my book before time to get the older ones in the bath. You got the checkbook balanced yet?" Balancin our checkbook was an art that had to be within the penny, as that's right where we lived.

"Nope. I've been banjaxed."

Bensy shook her head. "You can finish up after we feed all these youguns."

And so I did.

CHAPTER SEVENTEEN

The phone rung promptly at nine the next mornin. It was the lovely Mabel from Dr. Cutts office. "I'm callin about yore second sperm count gettin done. We got to reschedule it. Dr. Cutts done fell yesterday and broke his fool arm. Plus, he's got the flu, which is why he fell in the first place, I reckon, bein weak and all."

I was blushin plumb to my roots. I found it hard to discuss anything to do with sperm with Mabel. I'd already been through this humiliatin experience once, and they'd found zero sperm. I couldn't figure out why they wanted to do it again; even though Dr. Cutts had said it was still risky until six months from surgery.

"When?"

"Well, I don't know yet, didn't you hear me? I'm just a'callin to cancel the one you got next week. Think you can remember not to come?"

"That won't be a problem, Mabel." Actually, I'd forgotten about the appointment in the first place.

"Good. I'll call you when he comes back to work. Don't fergit to use pertekshun till after the test."

"Okay."

"Too bad he had to cancel. We got fresh *"Playboys"* in yesterday." She snickered and hung up.

"Have mercy." I mumbled as I hung up.

This whole thing was gettin way more'n ridiculous.

I'd no moren hung up the phone till it rung again. This time it was one of the Parker twins, (Tom, I think) askin about settin up a photo shoot and commercial video with the whole family and the van. He wanted the boys all dressed alike, and all the girls dressed alike. I was embarrassed to tell him we had no such outfits, nor a budget that could come up with a wardrobe.

He insisted that wouldn't be a problem, he'd call the department store downtown and tell them to charge it to their business and explain it was a commercial. He give me a phone number for Bensy to call and talk to the photographer, who would give advice about colors and design.

He wanted to do this next week, if our schedules allowed.

I told him I reckon we could, as far as I knowed.

I updated Bensy; she called the photographer and found out good schemes for our colorin. Sounded pretty Hollywood to me.

Since this was scheduled for first thing in the mornin, Bensy proceeded to make the babies' appointments for their check up with the pediatrician right after that. I wadn't sure it was a good idea, but her reasonin was they would be all dressed up so cute. Whatever; all I can say is, *women*! The plan was for me then to get Lilly Ann to preschool and me and Monte go home, as both mamas and Bensy's granny was goin to the pediatrician with Bensy.

Just as we started to leave the house, Ron called. He said he had some excitin information for me, and wanted to treat me to lunch. I told him I'd more than likely have Monte with me. His enthusiasm stalled, but after a minute, said he still had to see me, so come on anyhow.

I figured he musta won the lottery or somethin.

When we got to the photo shoot, the first thing they did was put people in charge of dressin the babies. Bensy dressed Lilly Ann, I dressed Monte and myself. He looked like my mini-me. They put make-up on Bensy and fixed her hair. I wadn't sure who she was when they got finished.

Then the hairdresser come over and 'mussed' my hair. I told him to stop or I was gonna muss his face.

The babies was brought back, Paula dressed just like her mama and Lilly Ann. That left the boys lookin like my mini-mini-mes.

I thought it was sappy.

They put us in front of the van and we stood there while the Parker twins talked about theirselves bein twins, and how we had a special place in their hearts, etc.

Then they motioned us, we waved, Bensy got in the van and

I started handin her babies. She laid them in their seats, hauled Monte up, and me and Lilly Ann climbed in. They stopped filmin so we could strap everbody in, then started up again as we drove off, wavin like lunatics.

I figured I better eat lunch with Ron today, because after this train wreck showed on TV, I'd never be able to go to town again.

After it was over, I loaded up Lilly Ann and Monte in the truck, kissed Bensy goodbye (they filmed that, too) and told her to be careful. I dropped Lilly Ann off at Day Care (motto: *Because we do!),* and Monte and me went on home for a few minutes. I wanted to check on the house and make sure Monte went potty before we headed out to town.

Granny pulled up in the yard about the same time I did. "I've come to take ker of Monte so you kin do suhum else with yore time." She hobbled over to me, finally straight by the time she got to me. "I'm as stiff as a corpse when I first try to stand up." She shook her head. "Old age is turrbul ugly."

"You think it's bad now, just wait till you spend time with this rounder." Monte grinned up at me.

"Shaw, that's what keeps me a'goin."

"It just so happens Ron has invited me to eat dinner in town. He says he's got some excitin news for me."

Granny raised her eyebrows. "That so? Well, by all means,

git." Then she squinted her eyes at me, really lookin at me. "What the devil is wrong with yore har? It's all messed up."

I groaned. "Big wind, I reckon."

We went on inside. "Let me get Monte to the potty before I go."

Monte was already strippin off his clothes. He peed, then I put a pull-up on him, just in case. He hadn't had any accidents in a week, but I thought to be on the cautious side when he was stayin with the elderly. He grabbed a sweatshirt and his helmet and a flashlight, and went flyin to Granny with another helmet, which she promptly put on. I handed her our good flashlight and told her to not let Monte con her out of it. His was a dollar flashlight; ours was for when the power went out.

Monte was a man on a mission. He ran back to his room, found the book he was lookin for, handed it to Granny and said, "Read."

It was his favorite book at the moment. It was all about miners, hence the gear.

They was all settled when I left.

Ron was already sittin down when I got there, but he was usually early for food, unless he was waylaid by cows. Ha!

He guffawed when he saw me. "Lord have mercy! Have you done gone to the other side?"

I frowned. "Huh?"

"Your hair is all doodled up and you're dressed fit to kill." He tilted his head. "Fact is; you're cute as a button."

Obviously, with all the Monte stuff, I'd forgot to unmuss my hair. I shook my head and sat down. "Life's hard when you are a superstar."

"Oh, yeah. How'd that go?"

"I'll be the laughinstock of town as soon as them commercials start airin, that's how it went."

Ron grinned. "In that case, I cain't wait to see it." He picked up the menu. "The chef ain't in today, so I think it's safe to eat here." He grinned. The regular cook was as far from a chef as you could get. She was a ornery old woman who burnt stuff too much and glared at you if you complained. She couldn't be fired 'cause she owned the place.

The waitress come and took our order; confirmin that Rosie wadn't there. She rolled her eyes and said, "John Henry is cookin today. Wish he'd cook ever day, but no, he's gotta lay sorry drunk at home." John Henry was Rosie's husband and a really fine cook.

As usual, I was dumbfounded at what-all Ron ordered.

She left, and Ron put his forearms on the table. "I think I may have the deal of the century for you."

"What do you mean?"

"I'm sure you remember my cattle rustlers."

"Yeah. Their fame will evermore be engraved on my heart."

Ron looked at me. "I thank you better comb your hair. It's startin to get to you."

"Sorry. What about 'em?"

"They discovered a great deal of cattle stolen by them Bronson boys. They've been able to return some to their owner; most of them, I think. But there's a few left. Sherriff's sure they are stole, too, but can't trace 'em. Anyway, the remainin cattle are gonna be auctioned off. Not many people know about it, and fewer than that care much. You, sir, might get some humdinger deals on fine cattle."

I felt my heart speed up. "I ain't got much money. But the bank might be willin to do a short term loan for somethin that promisin."

Ron nodded. "They probably would."

We ate like crazy men; me from excitement, Ron from bein his usual self.

"Why, hello, boys!" I looked to see where he was. Uncle Wend had snuck up on me.

"Hello, Uncle Wend."

He slapped me on the back. "And how are all your progeny today?"

At least I knowed this word. "They are doin good, Uncle Wend. In fact," I said, feelin myself grinnin, "I'd go as far as to say they are splendiferous."

Uncle Wend was silent for a moment, then threw back his head and laughed. He patted me on the shoulder. "That's my boy!" He chuckled again. "I'll be movin along, but Charlie?"

You know I hate bein called Charlie. "Yes, Uncle Wend?"

"You really need to do somethin with that hair of yours." He shook his head and walked off.

Ron batted his eyes at me. "I think you're as hot as a three dollar pistol."

"And I think you got a screw loose. I'm gettin outta here. Gonna go home and wash my durn hair."

"In the middle of the day, like a girl?"

"Whatever it takes. Will you let me know when you hear about the auction?"

"You know I will, buddy."

I batted my eyes at *him*. "And thank you so much for the food. It was *so* sweet of you."

I walked off in a hurry.

CHAPTER EIGHTEEN

When I got in the truck, I saw I had to stop and get gas. I wheeled in, hollered to Teeny, the woman that run the store. She waved, grinnin. As I started pumpin, two girls – maybe fourteen – come up to me with a piece a paper, a pen and the giggles. "Can I help ya'll?"

One of 'em, I think I recognized her from Youth at church, but couldn't place her name, stopped gigglin long enough to ask for my autograph. I grinned, lookin around for Ron. "Okay, girls, where is he?"

They looked a little confused. "Where's who?" the one I didn't recognize at all asked.

"Ron. He put ya'll up to this, didn't he?"

"Oh, no, honest Mr. Simpson! We saw you on the television commercial!" More gigglin. "You looked so *cute!* Why, you could be famous, maybe!"

I just stared at them. Had drugs come to our town? "Hand me the paper." I looked at it, smelled of it, (which brought on more confused looks), then started to sign it.

"Put *'to my best friend'* please." Boy, I thought how great that would go over with her daddy.

"I'm tryin to remember your name, honey. I ain't your best friend. Who's your daddy?"

She blushed. "I'm Elizabeth Hawthorn. My Daddy is Robert."

I nodded. "I remember now. Well, Elizabeth, how about I put *'from a good friend of the family'*?"

"Okay." She said reluctantly.

The other girl handed me her paper. "Just sign your name, I guess."

"You sure?"

"Well, I wanted you to put 'love, Charlie', but I guess you won't."

I hate bein called Charlie.

"You got that right. What's your name?"

"Just put 'to Sandy'." She looked disappointed.

When I went in to pay for my gas, Teeny was laughin her fat self about off her stool.

"Not funny, Teeny. Those girls need serious help."

That made her laugh harder.

Made me even grin a little.

"Hit's thu har," She advised me.

I begin to seriously consider a crew cut, if I knowed Bensy wouldn't kill me.

I walked in the door at the house to one excited woman. Bensy had watched the commercial over and over, and insisted I watch it immediately.

"I ain't too sure about watchin it at all."

"Why on earth not, Charles Simpson? It has your wife and children on there!"

I told her about the autograph seekers.

She hooted. "Well, you do look awful cute in that commercial. Come on, sit down and watch it with me."

It was just as I figured; I looked like a fool.

Before there was much time for comment, the phone rung. Bensy listened quietly, a very serious look on her face. She got up and got a pad and pen and began to take notes.

I started feelin a little alarmed. After all, the babies had been to the doctor that mornin. Did they find somethin wrong?

She thanked whoever had been jabberin on the other end and hung up, a dazed look on her face.

"What's wrong?"

"They ain't nothin wrong, Charles. That was some fella by the name of Dow Rutherford. He's a producer of some movie called *"The Happy Family Show"* and wants the babies to be in it. Well, maybe just the boys. He has to look at Paula to see if she resembles them enough."

"They have quads in the movie? And how the heck did he find out about our babies?"

"He saw the commercial. And no, not quads, but you can only have a baby on the set for so long, somethin about child labor laws. So, he'd swap 'em out till the scenes are done. He said he'd put us up in a nice hotel until the shoot was done."

"For how long?" I felt like *I* was in a movie or somethin.

"Anywhere from three to seven days. Dependin on how things go. We'd have free lodgins, free food, and the babies get paid. I reckon we could put it in savins for them." She looked at me closely. "But you're gonna say no, ain't you?"

I could feel myself startin to squirm. "No, I wadn't gonna say not to do it. Do you want to? Maybe your Mama could go with you. I cain't hardly see how I can miss work again. They've been mighty nice durin all this baby stuff, then the commercial stuff, but I don't know that they'd appreciate me bein off more."

"I know. I'd have to ask her." She tilted her head and looked at me square in the eye. "But there's more, ain't they?"

Woman read me like a book. "I was in a movie once," I blurted.

"What? When? And how did I miss that?" She crossed her arms over her chest, which ain't never a particularly good sign.

119

"I was just a baby. I knowed about it when I was little, then I sorta forgot about it some."

"What movie?"

"The name of the movie was *"The Real Christmas"*. We watched it ever year when it come on TV, then I guess it quit comin on ever year." I shrugged.

"Who did you play?"

"Um, baby Jesus."

Bensy got tears in her eyes! Women are so strange. She hugged me. "That's the sweetest thing I know about you."

Great. Somethin I don't remember, had no control over, and that's the sweetest thing about me. Don't say much for me, if you're askin.

"I need to talk to your mama and see how that all happened."

"Feel free. I'm hungry. Anything cooked?"

She was dialin the phone, so she just waved me toward the kitchen. Good enough for me. If she cooked, I would eat.

CHAPTER NINETEEN

I come home from work the next day to find Bensy wavin a DVD around. Seems my mama had ordered *"The Real Christmas"* some years ago when she found it had come out on DVD. She let Bensy borrow it until our own copy, which Bensy had ordered that mornin, come.

After supper, it was the most important thing on the agenda after we watched the commercial again. Lilly Ann and Monte both hollered out through the whole commercial, and Monte strutted around the room ever time he saw hisself on TV.

Bensy had promised they could stay up and see the video, to see 'Daddy star in a movie'. They had got ready for bed willinly with me coachin them while Bensy put the babies down to sleep.

"Scoop over, Daddy." Lilly Ann said, wigglin between me and the arm of the couch. "I wants to sits with ya."

I 'scooped' over, and we snuggled.

Of course, both of them was asleep before I made my début, as the baby doesn't enter the picture until near the end. I had my very own close up, too.

Bensy started gettin all weepy. "You was a beautiful baby, Charles. Look at that hair!"

I think the hair is what got me the part. I had a head full of dark curls, and long lashes to boot. I was a pretty baby, and played the part flawlessly.

Slept through the whole thing, till the very end, where, as if on cue, I opened my big old baby eyes and looked up into Mary's face.

Mama said they did it in one take I done so good.

After we wrangled sleepin toddlers into their beds, Bensy filled me in on the quads movie doins. "Mr. Rutherford will be in town next Wednesday afternoon. He'd like to come here to see the babies in their 'natural environment', he called it. He wants to bring a photographer with him. He said not to dress them up, in fact he preferred them to be in all white onesies, which I told him we could easily do. He doesn't want me to tell him which one is Paula, either." She turned to me. "He won't be here until six, so reckon you could get off a hour early and be here?"

"Yeah. Henry will let me come in early or stay late or somethin to make it up."

Bensy looked awful relieved. "They sound pretty uppity. I could tell he thinks I'm a slow witted country woman, just cause of my accent." She got a wicked gleam in her eye. "Maybe I'll invite Uncle Wend over and let him try to out talk him."

I threw back my head and laughed. "If it gets too snobby in here, that's just what we'll do."

122

****

When Dow Rutherford arrived he did put on airs some. But I figured it was because he was so danged nervous. Bensy was nervous, too, and that set the younguns to squallin. And I don't just mean the quads. Monte joined right in. If that don't make you nervous, well, you got nerves of steel.

I got Bensy and Monte a cup of milk and a cookie, which calmed her down some and sent Monte into bliss. When he stopped yowlin, the babies stopped, too.

That calmed Mr. Rutherford down a right smart.

I started feelin like a professional counselor or somethin.

Pretty soon, old Dow was holdin a baby in each arm, Bensy had one and I had Paula (although Dow didn't know that. Bensy had dressed them in all white, and had turned down the cuff of the socks, which was color coordinated to each baby so nobody got mixed up.)

He had a lot of questions about us findin out she was pregnant with four, the usual fascination everbody in the whole dang universe had, I reckon.

He looked at them with fascination, marvelin that he couldn't tell one from the other, even which one was the girl.

The photographer, Gill Peterson, was snappin pictures and takin video the whole time. Dow said when we saw the video it would be more tellin.

We watched the video with fascination. It was remarkable. They did look like carbon copies of one another. I could tell which one was Paula, though. She had pulled ahead a little in weight, and her face was shaped differently. Plus her hair was a little different color.

It didn't take Dow long to notice either. The photographer grinned. He'd seen the difference right off. "Is that the girl?"

"That's Paula." Bensy agreed.

"She's pretty close. Her hair is a different shade. But the boys truly are identical. It's fascinatin. They are exactly what we are lookin for."

Gill reached down to remove his disc and the "*The Real Christmas*" DVD fell to the floor. Dow reached down to pick it up. "What's this?" He sorta looked funny.

Bensy preened a little.

I rolled my eyes a little.

"That's the movie my husband starred in."

"What?" Dow asked, lookin at me with wide eyes.

"I didn't *star* in the movie."

"But you were in it? As an extra?"

"Well, not exactly-"

Bensy butted in. "He *was,* too, the star! I don't care what he says. He was the Baby Jesus."

By now Dow was lookin at me with somethin akin to awe. I was gettin extremely uncomfortable.

"Were you really, Charles? Baby Jesus, I mean."

"Yeah. Bensy didn't know about it until ya'll called us, then I said somethin about it, and Mama had the DVD, and well, there it is, in your hand."

"This is unbelievable." Dow stood up and raked his hands through his hair. He turned and looked at me. "Do you realize this is the movie that made me want to be in the business? I loved this movie when I was a kid so much it drove my parents nuts." He sat back down. "You were a beautiful baby, I'll say that much. I still watch it every Christmas. It's no wonder why they picked you. I bet you won hands down at the audition."

"That's what they say. You realize I have no memory of any of this. I liked it as a kid, too. I mean, I sorta knowed it was me, havin seen all the baby photo albums, but the connection is still not easy to do."

Dow laughed. "I feel like askin for your autograph. May do it yet!"

****

Dow hadn't been gone fifteen minutes when there was a

knock at the door. It was Uncle Wend and Aunt Marveena, dressed fit to kill. Uncle Wend's face fell when he saw we didn't have company. It was all I could do to play innocent and pretend they'd come to visit when I knowed they'd come to ogle the movie people.

Bensy saw right through them, too. But she didn't play quite as nice. She sat them down on the couch and give 'em two babies each to hold. They was a little overwhelmed. Especially when Monte come in to hug "Unca Wend!"

Uncle Wend asked Monte if he had on big girl *panties*. Monte assured him, "Nope. Got pulled ups. See?" Then he grabbed his pull ups, sayin, "Dey pulled up, and dey pulled down!" and dropped his britches.

Marveena gasped. Monte may have been only the second nude male she'd ever seen, assumin she's seen Uncle Wend, and please God don't take us there.

"The boy is becomin a hobbledehoy!" Uncle Wend gasped. I was sure it was the truth, whatever it meant.

The cats had already been circlin them, finally perchin on the couch back, watchin everthing with interest. Their faces was only inches from Uncle Wend and Aunt Marveena's. Aunt Marveena sneezed. Lilly Ann come flyin in when she heard the commotion Monte was makin, and Dancer come runnin in with her.

When Dancer jumped up on the couch between Uncle Wend

and Aunt Marveena, tryin to lick the babies' faces, Uncle Wend cried, "Zoomania!" and begged us to take the babies from them before they was eaten alive by "this rabid animal".

It was a shame they had to leave so soon.

CHAPTER TWENTY

Granny called me Saturday mornin for a ride. She said the new medications she'd been put on made her head feel all funny and she "wadn't wantin to drive."

"I'll be glad to, Granny. Where we goin?"

"That's my business."

"Well, I cain't very well drive you unless I know where we're goin."

"Don't fret about it. I'll tell you when we start. Just be here by quarter of three, I got to be there at three."

At least now I knowed her appointment was in town since Granny liked to get ever place early and was givin us only fifteen minutes.

I pulled up at her house and she was out the door like a rocket, not even givin me time to get out and open the door for her. She was clutchin a paper sack to her chest. When she got in the truck, she sat the sack down between us and I noticed it was taped at the top.

"Whatcha got there?" I asked.

"This here is what I'm takin to Bill Drennon."

"You sayin we're goin to the *funeral home?*" I squirmed a little. "Are you feelin all right?" I looked at her closely. She looked fine to me.

"Well, I got up from my deathbed again and fried up some chicken."

"Then why are we goin to see the undertaker?"

"I had your mama buy me some new drawers the last time she went to the Dollar Store. They was twisted in the seams and they'll peench ye whur a girl don't wanter be peenched; at least in a unfriendly way."

"Granny!" I blushed plumb purple. "Are you tellin me Bill Drennon wears women's underwear?" She had embarrassed me two ways at once. That was a record, even for my granny.

I mean, really? An undertaker in women's underwear? That was too much.

"Lord, no! What's wrong with you?" she looked at me like *I* was the crazy one in this conversation. "Bill and me was just talkin the other day down at the doctor's office in the waitin room – he's had the bronchitis – and it come up about how poor old May Rogers' daughter had to go to Walmart in the middle of the night to buy her mama some new underwear afore they dressed her to go in the coffin. I reckon you know no woman would want *used* underwear to be buried in, don't you?"

"Well, I ain't never thought about it, to tell you the truth; and I don't see what difference it'd make."

She shook her head in disgust. "Ain't no tellin what kinda

rags I'll be buried in if your mama goes first."

"Granny, I promise you: if I have to get you buried, I'll buy you new drawers."

"That's some comfort, anyhow." She said. "I'm a'takin these new underpants to him for them what's goin to be layin a corpse. They shore won't feel no peench from the seams."

"Wait a minute. You just said they ought not to have used underwear, but you are takin him used underwear."

"Don't be a fool. I'm takin Bill them that I ain't never took outta the pack. How many par do you think it took me to figger out they wadn't worth buyin? One was enough."

"So what are you gonna do with the pair you done wore?"

"I'll keep 'em and wear 'em in a peench." Realizin her pun, she cackled and slapped me on the arm.

I shook my head, cranked up and off we went to the funeral home. I didn't go in; I didn't figure I had no place in the conversation.

Goin back home, I had the radio on low, and all of a sudden Granny turned up the volume. One of our local boys had made hisself a CD and they played it on the local station.

"Lord, will you listen to that! Hearin that boy sang is like water to a parched throat. And have you seen him in person?" She asked. "Why he looks so clean he purely shines."

"I do believe you've got yourself a crush on that boy."

She smiled at me. "I do believe yore right. Now, hush. I want to hear this here song."

We drove the rest of the way home in silence.

****

Monte's birthday, Lilly Ann's birthday, Bensy's birthday, and my birthday all are in October, which was why it was so nice the other four of us waited until April to be born.

Anyway, both families usually got together to celebrate all our birthdays around mid-October, figurin it'd hit all of them pretty close.

That was always truly an adventure, and usually one of the main gifts we received was babysittin promises so Bensy and me could go out on a childless date to celebrate alone.

This year was no different. Our budget was a lot tighter than before, so we decided to go to a nice restaurant but have a salad with water only. That way we'd get the ambiance without the big price ticket.

We dressed fit to kill, and Bensy even talked me into lettin her fix my hair like it was for the TV commercial, because she said it was sexy. I didn't like it, but she did and sometimes you have to consider lookin like a fool to please your wife.

We'd ordered our salad and water and while eatin it we actually thought of somethin to talk about besides kids. Suddenly the waiter appeared and placed two plates in front of us, both filet mignon, baked potato and some steamed veggies. My mouth watered and I think I heard a small scream escape my wallet.

"Sir, you've delivered this to the wrong table." A tear formed in my eye and I had to death grip my hands to keep one from grabbin the steak knife and the other the fork.

He smiled. "No sir. Compliments from another diner. They asked me what you'd ordered and when I told them they insisted ya'll needed more than that just to keep your strength up. I think they was goin to treat you to dessert until they was told you didn't have anything but salad."

Bensy asked who, but the waiter declined to say.

What can you do? We ate like pigs.

On the way home, we tried to figure out who in thunder who do that for us, but the strange thing was we come up with so many names of folks who had been so kind to us, we determined it could be anybody with a pocket book.

We decided to just enjoy it and be thankful.

Lilly Ann went around for days tellin everbody she knowed that she was now "Four years old and one day", then "Four years old and two days", etc. till we finally told her to say four or nothin at all.

Monte tried to be like her and puff his chest out and say proudly, "I three." But by "I three and two days", he was bored with that, and he give it up.

I tried to convince Bensy to be like Lilly Ann but she just punched me in the arm.

Halloween's arrival finally swept the birthdays plumb off the radar for the kids as they become obsessed with who they was goin to be and how much candy they was goin to get.

We dressed the quads up like little bumblebees and took their pictures. Bensy found some really ugly black and yellow striped t-shirts and wrote "queen bee" on the front of hers and "drone" on mine. She found two sets of bug antennae that we smushed on our heads. We carried the babies to the door so folks could make over them. I had one daddy with three little ones in tow look at my shirt and mutter, "That's the truth, brother," before turnin away. Made me want to ask where the little woman was, but I was afraid to. He looked none too happy and I'm sure he really did feel like a drone.

The quads slept through a lot of the trick or treatin. Mama brung Lilly Ann and Monte back from a short trick or treatin in town. We run out of candy so we turned off the lights. We was listenin to the chatter of Lilly Ann and Monte about their trip and goin over their candy stash when the phone rung.

It was Ron. Mara was in labor. He'd just come in with the twins from trick or treatin when her water broke. His parents was on a trip and Mara's parents was nowhere to be found. He was in a panic. "I hate to ask you, but would ya'll take the twins while I get Mara to the hospital?"

I thought I might have me a panic attack, right there. Them little fellers was as hell bent on destruction as any demolition crew I'd ever come across. Bensy had been standin there and heard him ask. Her eyes got big and she grabbed aholt of the counter like she might faint.

"Of course, Ron. You know we'll be glad for them to stay the night, if that's what you need. Do you want me to come get them?"

"No, we ain't got time. I'll swing by and drop them off on our way." I heard a click as he hung up.

"What have we ever done that was so bad that we have ours and theirs, all on a sugar high right before bedtime?" Bensy whined. "Put up the fine china and hide the cats."

"We ain't got fine china and the cats are on their own," I grumped.

It was what we expected, and more.

Ron was beside hisself when he called at three a.m. (like I needed to be woke up) whoopin and hollerin because Mara had delivered them a nine pound baby girl.

Old Ron got what he prayed for.

Little did he know Melissa, as they named her, would be a ring leader in terror herself as soon as she was able to walk.

Sometimes you just can't catch a break.

CHAPTER TWENTY-ONE

Granny caught me just before I walked out the door to work. Bensy handed me the phone. All Granny wanted was to let me know she was in need of a loaf of bread if by chance I'd be goin by a store on my way home and had the time to waste on the likes of her.

That's what she said. I swan, I don't know why that woman can't just come out and say what she wants: Bring me a loaf of bread on your way home.

Anyway, I grabbed a loaf and took it straight to her house that evenin. I'd just got in the door and laid the loaf on the counter so me and granny could begin the great negotiations of who was payin for the dang bread. She also wanted to add twenty dollars for my time and gasoline. I might have spent three minutes in the store and spent a nickel's more in gas, which I told her. She opened her mouth to commence her side again when Mama come bargin in like the tail end of a tornado.

I noticed she had a loaf of bread tucked under her arm.

She barely acknowledged me and altogether ignored my loaf of bread as she set hers down beside it.

I wondered how many more people Granny had told she needed a loaf of bread.

Lookin at Granny, she said, "Here's your bread." Without takin a breath, she announced, "I just found out Sister

Merriweather died."

"Shut your mouth!" Granny exclaimed. "What in the world happened?"

I leaned up against the counter. From experience, I knowed this would take a while.

"They ain't even told she was dead till just now on account of her baby sister from up in Tennessee didn't know. Baby sister Lizzie has Facebook and all, so they knowed she'd see it before it could be told to her proper if *anybody* knowed." She shook her head. "Anyhow; the family went to pick Sister up for church yesterday. When she didn't come on out to the car, they used Brother's copy of her house key to get in."

"Don't tell me Brother was the one what found her!"

"Lord, no," Mama said, "He cain't hardly make it up steps no more. Bev went in – said she hollered for her granny but they wadn't no answer – you know Sister can't hear good a'tall – so Bev went on through the house. Sister was still in the bed. And no wonder Sister didn't hear Bev, for she was dead."

"Land's sakes." Granny took a deep breath. "Well, at least her own boy didn't find her."

"Wait." I said. "I'm confused. Is Brother Sister's brother?"

Granny looked at me, annoyed. "Of course not. Brother is

Sister's oldest boy. Names Harold. All the other younguns after him called him Brother and it stuck."

"Well," I asked, "Then what was Sister's real name?"

Mama and Granny studied on that a minute. Granny spoke. "Well, now, that could *be* her real name. I don't recall no other. She was number sixteen of sixteen children, so they maybe run out of names by the time they got to her."

That sounded familiar.

"Sixteen! Good grief! And here I thought Bensy and me had it bad."

Mama give me one of them 'don't be smart with me' looks and turned back to Granny. "They was real worried about Brother's heart. You know he ain't been the same since Sis died."

Granny nodded sadly.

"Who's Sis?" I asked. I couldn't help myself.

"She was Brother's wife."

I could tell they was both gettin tired of me. I was used to it, and not as scared as I used to be. "So, was her given name really Sis?"

Granny set in, "No, that weren't her given name. Her mama had bad mental problems; in fact she was in the lunatic asylum when she had Sis. Fer years everbody thought she was just plain crazy, but turned out it was a brain tumor. She died when Sis was about eight months old. Had a old maid aint raise her. But to answer yore question, her give name was Jezebel Scarlett."

"Oh. Sorry to hear that. Sis sounds fine. So, when did Sis die?"

Mama said, "Probably sixty years ago, or more."

This puzzled me, a little. "How old is Brother?"

Granny said, "Sommers around my age – eighty-two or three, I reckon."

"And we're talkin his *mama* just died *unexpectedly*?" I heard my voice go up a little.

"Well, we are *tryin* to talk about it." Granny's eyes was gettin all squinty and I could tell she was gettin mad at me for interruptin so much.

Mama put her hands on her hips. "Charles, are you gettin feeble minded? That's what we been talkin about this whole time."

I scratched my head. "I'm afraid to ask, but, how old was Sister Merriweather?"

Granny beamed. "Just celebrated her one hundurd and thurd birthday."

One more question, I thought, just one more. "And the

family was *shocked* that she died?"

Mama and Granny shook their heads sadly.

"It was awful shockin," Granny sighed heavily.

Mama agreed.

****

I've always been told you can't pick your family, but you can pick your friends. Meanin, I suppose, that as crazy as that conversation was, they was family and I had to live with it.

Then answer me how come my friend's conversations are just as crazy – or maybe crazier – than my family's? I mean, what does that say about me?

I had no more than got home when Ron called. I've had a lot of very odd conversations with this man, we go back a long way. But I do believe this one took the cake.

At least, so far.

I'd set in to tell Bensy about Sister, Brother and Sis. She'd already started glazin over when the phone rung.

"Hey, Buddy, what's up?" I wanted to sound as cheerful as possible because I figured him and Mara wadn't gettin no sleep, havin those wild ape twins and a newborn.

"Hey. Charles, I need you to do me a favor."

I'd had a long day, and I was tired. I knowed Bensy needed me, too. But what can you do?

Glancin at Bensy, I asked Ron, "Whatcha need?"

"Um, I need you to bring me some pants."

"Okay…where are you to need me to bring you pants?" I glanced at Bensy and when she heard what I asked, she sat right down by me.

"I'm in the parkin lot of the beauty shop where I get my hair cut, and they're all starin at me."

"Who's starin at you?"

"All the women in the shop. Workers and customers alike."

"They can *see* you don't have on pants?"

He sounded shocked. "No! Of course not! Lord, Charles! I've got Mara's apron over my lap."

"The frilly one with pink flowers?" I grinned.

"In my predicament, it don't matter what it looks like."

"Just out of curiosity, why don't you have on pants? Was it too hot to put 'em on when you left the house?" I was really enjoyin this.

He sighed loudly. "No. I went back to work today and spilled a big can of oil on my pants just before I was gettin in the car. So I slipped 'em off and threw 'em in the back all wadded up in a bag so the oil wouldn't get on anything. Mara'd kill me if I got oil on the inside of this car. Anyway, I threw them all the way in the back, so I cain't reach 'em. As I started down the road I noticed I had no gasoline in this car. At all. I don't even see how it cranked up."

I laughed out loud. "You, Mr. Always-have-at-least-half-a-tank had no gas."

"We've had a few rough days, okay? Plus my nephew drove it to run errands a few times. I forgot about it."

"How'd the beauty shop get involved in all this? How would they know you don't have on pants?"

"Just as I saw that my gage was sittin on past empty, my cell phone rung and it was Pam remindin me of my hair cut appointment in fifteen minutes. I look like a sheep dog."

"And you said, '*Well, Pam, I don't have on pants*'?" Bensy was snickerin by now.

"Ron, just shut up and let me tell it." He took a big breath. "I told her I didn't know what I was gonna do – I was really panickin, I'm tellin you – told her I was out of gas and why I didn't have on pants. Of course, she laughed at me, but said she'd meet me at the station and pump some gas for me and I could go on home."

"So, how –"

"Just let me finish this sorry tale, okay? Just as I started past the beauty shop the car started stutterin and I knowed I better coast in and stop. I figured I could yell at Pam as she come out, and she could follow me to the gas station. But when I parked, Pam's car was gone. And all these women are standin and starin and laughin at me at through the plate glass winder which I'm parked in front of."

"I guess she shared your plight before she took off to the gas station."

"I reckon. So, I'm stuck. Outta gas, no pants, and in front of a winder full of women."

"Ron, you seem to have a problem holdin onto your pants."

"Are you gonna help me or not? I ain't got nobody else to call. Mara cain't leave -"

"Yeah, yeah, I'll help. Just keep your pants – never mind. I got some big old sweat pants I think you can squeeze into. And I'll bring a can full of gas. Sit tight."

I hung up and Bensy and me howled.

Aint' good friends a wonderful thing?

CHAPTER TWENTY-TWO

Mid-November, early on a Friday mornin, someone knocked on our door. Now, this is a time of pure chaos at our house - breakfast for everone, the cats and dog settin prayerfully under the table waitin for a morsel to drop, Lilly Ann chatterin nonstop and Monte usually, half asleep, upset about something.

I opened the door and there stood our neighbor, Tandy Burton. I turned red. "Miz Tandy I plumb forgot about returnin the cat carrier." It had been two months and it still sat in the hall closet, patiently waitin.

She come on in the house and laughed. "I cain't imagine why you'd forget anything." The babies had stopped eatin and was all starin at her, as was Monte and Lilly Ann. Dancer stood up suddenly and bonked her head on the table, as she was layin under it. The cats didn't bother movin, except their eyes, tryin to judge if anyone would notice if they grabbed food off the table since there was a distraction.

"Come on in and eat breakfast with us," Bensy said as she headed to the livin room. "It's one you won't forget."

Tandy shook her head. "That would be the truth, honey. But I cain't stay. I've got to get Precious to the vet. I think she's got a ear infection, and I figured since I was headed that way, I'd take the kitten I kept and get the next immunization that's due. That's when I realized I had lent ya'll the other carrier."

"You shoulda called me," I told her. "I'd brung it right over."

"I know you would have. But I imagined what was goin on at your house, and let me tell you, my imagination isn't good enough."

She walked over and cooed over the food encrusted babies, petted Dancer on the head, waved to Lilly Ann and shook hands with Monte.

Red come and wound hisself around her leg. "They sure are gettin big." She turned to me. "How did those boys behave at the vet?" She bent down and stroked the cat's fur.

Bensy and me looked at each other, frantic. "Um, well, the truth is, we ain't took 'em to the vet."

"Oh, my! These boys are gonna be trouble if you don't. Honey, they'll start markin their territory in here and it'll stink worse than any skunk you've met." She counted on her fingers. "Lord, they are already four months old. It's a wonder they aren't already doin it."

Well, that put the fear in me. "I reckon I'll go to the store today and buy carriers on my lunch break. Bensy can make the appointments."

Tansy raised a brow. "And when in tarnation will you have time to take them?"

Bensy and me looked at each other. I smiled weakly. "I

guess we'll figger it out."

Tandy thought a minute. "I tell you what. You buy those carriers. Make the appointment for day after tomorrow and I'll take them for you."

We started to protest. She held up her hand. "Let me tell you somethin. There's been times when I needed a helpin hand. I've often received it. I've got lots of time now, and I want to do this for ya'll. After all, what are good neighbors for?"

That's how Miz Tandy Burton took Red and Panda to the vet and got 'em fixed. The vet kept them till the next mornin so they could sober up because of all our younguns. They didn't charge us extra, accordin to Tansy.

But I think she fibbed. I think she paid the extra.

Like she said, she was a good neighbor.

****

Thanksgivin is usually the biggest family get together we have. Usually on Thanksgivin Day we all go to my granny's and the next day we all go to Bensy's granny's. It works that way because Bensy has some out of town family and it's easier for them.

Well, obviously, *we* was now in Granny's house. Our old house that Granny lived in wadn't nowhere big enough to hold my family; and my mama's house wadn't all that big either. Mama approached me about it right after Halloween.

She said she was afraid it would be too much on Bensy, but she didn't know where else we could do such. She didn't want to mention it to Bensy before she run it by me first, thinkin I might know what to do.

I ain't so good at mullin stuff over because I usually leave that up to Bensy. I told Mama all I knowed to do was ask. So I hollered at Bensy to come out on the porch when she could, which was pretty quick. The boys was down for a nap and Paula was the only one decidin she could do without and just be fussy. Mama promptly took her granddaughter and started swingin her. It seemed to calm them both – because Mama had worked herself up about askin – she looked as fretful as Paula.

"Everbody's wonderin if we can have Thanksgivin dinner here like always."

Bensy raised her eyebrows. "Do I have to cook?"

Mama spoke up. "Just the turkey. My mama will fix the dressin and bring it to cook in your oven. She'll send somebody, prob'ly me, to get the broth from the turkey early in the mornin. Everbody says they are willin to bring the rest. We'll make do with paper plates and such this year, so all the cleanup will be fairly easy."

Bensy shrugged. "Sounds good to me. I'd do more, but it's hard enough to get a meat and two vegetables on the table now."

"Oh, honey, don't I know it. You cain't possibly be nothin but tard."

Bensy sighed. "I'm wore out all the time." She smiled down at Paula. "But it's a little better'n it was."

Bensy asked the group of Sunday School girls that babysat sometimes if they'd come so she could clean the house. Well, them girls did better than that; they come *and* helped clean the house. There was six of them, so they helped do a little bit of everthing. We fed them pizza and they was happy.

Thanksgivin Day was a little on the chaotic side. Uncle Wend insisted on sayin the blessin (we all started prayin right then). Everbody that didn't have a baby in their arms joined hands.

Darlin Monte wrapped hisself around Uncle Wend's leg and looked up at him adorinly while Uncle Wend pretended Monte wadn't there.

He cleared his throat and began, "Dear Lord God in Heaven, we feel your ubiquitous self right here amongst us, from the highest to the lowliest of us present. Bless this food and thankyouforit. Amen."

Everone looked up in surprise. We'd all got sorta comfortable, expectin a long winded tribute to hisself disguised as talkin to God. When I opened my eyes, I saw the reason Uncle Wend had gone from his orator's voice to a quick amen.

Monte was lickin his shoes.

****

The rest of the day was uneventful. Everone ate till they was stuffed to the point of pain. The babies was all wallered near to death, Lilly Anne had recited everthing she could possibly remember from her preschool class, and Monte had announced loudly, mid-meal, he had to poop and would do so in the big boy bathroom.

Which was a relief all around.

Both the grannies and the mamas swept in and swooped up food, wrappin what pitiful leftovers they was, filled three garbage bags full of paper products and such, and left the kitchen close to spotless.

That night we had a bit of trouble gettin all the younguns to sleep. The babies had been held too much and was fretful. (Granny warned, "Them babies is gonner be sore. Don't be surprised if they's ill as hornets.")

Lilly Anne and Monte was wound up, too.

But Bensy and me was asleep by the time our heads hit our pillows.

Thanksgivin will do that to you.

CHAPTER TWENTY-THREE

We have a rule in our family that is never allowed to be broke. And that is: *No* Christmas doins until the day after Thanksgivin, unless I am awake enough on Thanksgivin evenin to untangle lights.

We tried our best to decide the best kind of tree for this year. We knowed the quads wadn't goin to be no trouble as they wadn't big enough to move too awful much on their own. They was just beginnin to scoot a little.

Monte had demolished a tree last year. It's a wonder it didn't kill him when it fell on him, but that's a long story, and you can probably imagine it all anyhow.

Lilly Ann is beyond such; she's more interested in what's under the tree now.

But we had a dog and two cats this year.

I was really worried about the cats.

Bensy and me decided a fake tree was in order for the next few years. Maybe when the quads was old enough to leave the tree alone and we was brave enough to see what the cats would do, maybe then we'd get a live tree again.

Bensy's granny got all upset over it. My granny shrugged. She'd had a little silver tree since the 1960's, and let me tell you, it wadn't nothin to brag about. It wadn't the first year she bought it, and it become the most pitiful thing I ever seen.

Since the kids was all still real little, we decided a five-footer was plenty tall enough. They'd still see it as a big tree, and it would be less for us to deal with, especially if the cats misbehaved.

Before we shopped for the tree, we put the expensive nativity set up on the mantel, and the cheap plastic one on the table so they kids could look, touch, rearrange, etc.

One mornin I found baby Jesus on the roof of the manger with the camel and a lamb. Monte explained "We don't got no reindeer".

We also put the wreath on the front door, lights across the porch, the tin Santa wavin in the yard and a basket of holly on the steps.

By December first, the tree was up. We let Lilly Ann and Monte decorate what they could reach. Lilly Ann kept at it, but Monte got bored after about three ornaments and decided to "set and watch". Dancer come over and laid down next to Monte. Monte laid down on top of the dog, and they both was asleep in a minute.

Granted, the tree was heavy on decorations at the bottom due to Lilly Ann's generous hand, but when the lights was turned on, it looked pretty good.

The cats both entered the room, and when they saw the tree, they froze. They continued in stalker mode, bellies low to the ground as they approached it.

I waited until they was right up at it, and blew the air horn.

They fuzzed up to twice their size, Monte woke up howlin because Dancer had jumped plumb off the floor into the next room, makin Monte's head bounce on the hardwood.

I don't know if I've ever said this, but I consider myself a great daddy, except on occasions such as this.

But my goal was met. The cats didn't go near the tree the whole time it was up.

Well, almost.

****

This year, goin to see Santa Claus was put into a whole new realm. We didn't just have a toddler and a preschooler. We had a whole clan.

We knowed the quads wouldn't remember this year, but we couldn't find it in us to take Lilly Ann and Monte to see Santa and leave the quads at home, or even take them at a different time. Neither seemed right.

The first Sunday that December, as we was pilin everbody up in the van to go home from church, Sam Carter hollered at me to come there a minute.

Sam was a heavyset man in his sixties, and as I went to him, I noticed he'd let his hair grow out and was growin a beard.

All white, both. I ain't stupid. It dawned on me he was goin to go about Santa business this year.

He was grinnin like a possum when I walked up. "Howdy, Santa," I said, grinnin right back.

He threw his head back and ho, ho, hoed.

Really.

He slapped me on the back and asked how was we gonna get all them younguns in old Santy's lap at once.

"That's what we've been tryin to figger out. I want it done all at once, not piece mill." I cocked my head at him. "Got any ideas?"

"Well, as a matter of fact, I have." Turns out the senior Sunday School class had been workin on Sam for about six weeks to convince him to be a Santa, mainly because we'd need him.

He finally agreed because the department store took one look at him and hired him on the spot. He said it was a good deal of Christmas spendin money that he hadn't counted on.

The park in the middle of town had a giant Christmas tree, with lit up reindeer on one side and a beautiful nativity on the other.

Sam had got permission to set up his 'Santa Chair' right in front of the tree on Saturday mornin next. It wadn't goin to be advertised, and he wanted us there early so we could get our pictures took without drawin a lot of attention. He said if anybody showed up durin, he'd let them take pictures, too, but he wadn't stayin.

Poor Sam.

Just gettin set up started bringin attention to him, large, fur trimmed, and red as he was. By the time we pulled up a few minutes later, there was already a dozen or so people standin around, watchin.

We got Monte photographed with Santa by hisself first, then Lilly Ann. When we started totin out baby after baby, people was on their cell phones quickern you can say jack rabbit, and by the time we'd got to photos of all the kids together, they was fifty people or so gathered. We counted: Each child individually snapped, check. All kids together, check. Bensy and me with kids, check. And just for kicks and giggles, we got one of me in Sam's lap, and then one of Bensy (showin a little leg) in his lap.

As we loaded up younguns left and right, Sam had him a line that went all the way around the park.

He looked at us and winked.

Can't blame him. Lots of the waitin customers was pretty good lookin women.

****

I shoulda knowed Mama was up to somethin as she was bein

awful eager to get Bensy and me out the door the day we wanted to shop for the kids. She even made us leave before Wincy got there to help out.

Bensy and me had a easy time of shoppin. We got stockin stuffers for the babies, Lilly Ann and Monte, and two toys each. Lilly Ann and Monte both was adamant about what they wanted, and we found it. I couldn't hardly believe it had been so easy.

Feelin a little guilty about it, we was goin to go to the storage buildin and pull out a few toys for the babies that had never seen the light of day. They got so much at the shower months ago, we didn't have anywhere to put the extra toys. We figured they'd be new to all of us.

We each went our separate ways for half a hour to shop for each other, then met for lunch at a restaurant.

I felt like a teenager. I knowed Bensy wanted this cute little outfit she'd been eyin. She'd lost baby weight (again) and was eager for somethin new. I got the outfit and found a necklace I liked real good and thought she would, too.

Since she looked like the cat that swallowed the little yellow bird, I guessed she'd found whatever it was she wanted to get me, too.

When we got home, I had to wait on a big van to pull out of our drive way before I could pull in. The guy drivin waved merrily, but kept on goin.

Bensy and me looked at each other, shrugged, made sure our trunk and doors was locked where all the goodies was, and entered the house.

Mama, Bensy's mama, both grannies, Bensy's best friend, Wincy – oh, what the heck- half the town was standin in my livin room surrounded by more stuff that I could take in.

Diapers, washin detergent, soap, shampoo, toothpaste, new toothbrushes, toilet paper, paper towels, dog food, cat food, lots of new clothes in bigger sizes for the kids, and on and on.

Bensy sat down and cried. I sat down and nearly cried.

Wow.

Nothin outdid this the rest of Christmas.

Even seein Lilly Ann as an angel and Monte as a cow (it had horns, so he kept sayin he was a reindeer) didn't touch me like that day.

Good folks, our friends.

****

December twenty-third: The evenin we did our good deed for the year. We invited Uncle Wend and Aunt Marveena for supper. Mama even made a coconut cake for us, because that was Uncle Wend's favorite dessert. That was a small price for Mama to pay, to keep from havin him to eat at *her* house. Bensy and me had cooked a roast with taters, carrots and onions with Granny's home canned green beans on the side. I made the cornbread and Bensy made the biscuits.

We invited them over so their arrival was after the babies was in bed, figurin it would be a easier meal without four babies at the table.

We had preached to Lilly Ann and *especially* Monte about good table manners. It ain't like they wadn't taught that already, but we figured a refresher course wouldn't hurt.

Uncle Wend seemed pleasantly surprised that Monte didn't act like his usual monkey-self at the table, and to tell the truth, I was probably more surprised than Uncle Wend.

Uncle Wend, of course, hogged most the conversation, but not as much as usual because he was shovelin food in his face as fast as possible.

He told Bensy she had certainly 'titivated herself up for the evenin. Bensy blushed and adjusted her blouse. I squinted, excused myself for a moment, ran to the bedroom and looked up the word on the laptop. I come flyin back into the livin room and slipped paper into Bensy's hand, where I'd written down the meanin of 'titivate'. She smiled.

Then she turned to Marveena and when the moment was right, she said, "Why, Marveena, I believe you, too, have titivated yourself up for the evenin."

Aunt Marveena adjusted *her* blouse.

Sometimes you just can't win.

We sat back after the meal, enjoyin coffee and coconut cake in the livin room. Lilly Ann was colorin in her Christmas colorin book, and Monte was usin his Legos to build some strange thing that only a three-year-old can understand.

Whatever it was, it caught Uncle Wend's eye. "Why, what's that you're buildin there, my boy?" he asked.

Monte studied his work for a moment. Then he shrugged. "I don't know if you don't know."

We all laughed. Uncle Wend smiled fondly (Yes, it's hard to believe. I guess it's because it was so close to Christmas) at Monte. "He certainly has a gelogenic personality, doesn't he?"

We all smiled and nodded, Monte especially. I thought his head might fall off he was noddin so hard. Monte knows a compliment when he hears one.

I hope.

Lilly Ann politely stopped her colorin when Aunt Marveena asked what Santa was bringin her for Christmas. Lilly Ann explained she wadn't sure about all of it, but certainly felt he would fulfill her wishes for a play kitchen and some dishes and pots and pans.

I felt relieved she hadn't changed her mind.

Monte now wanted a real, life-size dump truck and

'wrasslin' lessons.

Uncle Wend started to explain how that couldn't happen for a little boy, but Bensy stopped him in wide eyed panic. "Oh, Uncle Wend, we just never know what Santa will do, do we? And, why, there is another whole day before Christmas and some people change their mind. Over and over." She looked at him hard.

"Oh. Well, er, yes, of course." He grinned at Monte. "There is a world of wonder about old Santa. He'll come through for you."

The tears that was brimmin dried up, and Monte looked relieved.

As did the rest of us.

Monte has changed his mind about thirty times in three days. We knowed he'd be happy as slop come Christmas mornin, as long as no one denied him a wishful thought before then.

Finally, as Lilly Ann and Monte was both fallin asleep on the floor, Uncle Wend stretched and said they must soodle home. "It's a mild night, and we thought the walk would do us good."

"All the way to your house?" Was he really crazier than I thought? They lived a good five miles away.

"Oh, no, dear boy! Just to the far end of your driveway."

"Well, then, soodle away!" I cried.

"I must say I have spent this evenin in languid oblectation. Thank you both so much!"

Aunt Marveena hugged Bensy, then me. "I've had a lovely evenin, too. We'll return the favor soon."

We bid them good night, fell against each other and didn't move for a moment.

"I guess we orght to soodle on to the kitchen and get it cleaned up a little." I told Bensy.

She giggled. "You soodle. As for me, I'm racin to the bathroom. Too much coffee!"

And off she went.

****

We always spent Christmas Eve with my family. This year, of course, we'd be at our house.

Gettin the bigger house wadn't always to our advantage, we was findin out this holiday season.

We'd put a big old ham in the oven that mornin and everbody else was bringin the fixins.

Mama and Daddy had walked in the kitchen with their stuff, and Granny had walked back in the livin room and sat down for a minute. Monte crawled up in her lap yappin about what Santa was bringin him.

Somebody tapped on the front door. I heard Granny say,

"God in Heaven!" as she nearly pitched Monte to the floor in her rush to get up and fling open the door.

It was Tate Graham, my daddy's baby brother, and only siblin.

Nobody'd heard a peep from Tate Graham for over five years. There was eighteen years difference between Daddy and Tate Graham, and to say he had been an unexpected baby was an understatement.

He was a change of life baby who nearly died at birth, and afterwards for the rest of his childhood, nearly babied to death.

It didn't fare well for his adulthood, which he never could seem to quite reach and grab a'hold of.

Granny often said, "When Tate Graham was born, the doctor told me that baby had a lot of brains in his head. That puffed me up like a proud peacock. What I failed to understand was that the doctor didn't guarantee that he'd actually put his big brain into *use*."

He never did, neither. He flunked out of college that Granny was payin for. Twice. He failed job after job for not showin up. He could get a job real easy because he was a smooth interviewer, and people seemed eager to fall for big servins of b.s., which Tate Graham could spoon out all day long. But keepin a job was a whole different ballgame.

Off and on (more on than off, if you ask me), Granny had

rescued Tate Graham from financial disaster, once even bailing him out of jail for some such. But about five years ago he called again, askin for somethin. I happened to hear her end of the conversation. She told him, "Tate Graham, I have loved you to near destruction. As of now I am no longer available for anything but to receive and return our love. I will no longer put anything in the hand you hold out except my own. No more rescuin, no more savin, no more gittin you outta whatever you have got into. I'll take yore visits anytime. I'll send ye birthday cards if you tell me where yore at. But I'm done, son."

He hung up. We'd heard nary a word from him since, until right that minute as he stood on the other side of the door.

Granny flung open the door and Tate Graham said, "Mama, can I come in?"

She yanked his arm near plumb out of the socket. "I ain't got a ring nor a robe nor a fatted calf, but we got some other fine vittles fer ye to eat."

He hugged her up, eyes squeezed shut. When he opened them, he saw all of us. He blinked in surprise.

"Who do all these children belong to?"

"Bensy and me."

He took in Monte, who stood there with his pacifier half in his mouth, starin and Lilly Ann with her head cocked and her hands on her hips, lookin fierce. Then he saw one baby, then two, then – well, you know – and he forgot to speak proper and fell back into usin his mother tongue, Appalachian.

"Lord have mercy! All *four* of 'em?"

I nodded.

"And these other two?"

I nodded.

He sat down, hard. I was grateful he'd made it over to the couch, or else he'd a hit the floor.

My daddy walked into the room, propped hisself up against the door frame, just out of Tate Graham's reach. "Lots happens when you ain't heard from in five years."

Tate Graham. "John." He nodded at my daddy. "It sure can." He nodded again. "Congratulations to you all. Quite a crop of babies." He grinned, but nobody grinned back.

He looked at Granny. "I know you think I haven't called because I was angry with you. And at first, I was. But that phone call opened my eyes, Mama. I looked at myself. *Really* looked. And I didn't like who I saw. A kid in a grown man's body. So I did somethin about it. I enrolled in college, worked my way through and got a teachin degree. I wanted to make somethin of myself before I showed back up on your doorstep." Then his eyes got wide again. "I swear, I'm losin my mind. There's someone with me, and I forgot!"

He jumped up and run out the door. We all looked at each other. Granny was tremblin, but smilin, too.

"Guard your heart, Mama." My daddy said softly.

"Don't worry none, Son. I know." Granny looked at him, then turned as Tate Graham come back through the door.

He had a woman with him, I reckoned to be around forty, a good nine years younger than him, if not more. And in her arms was a baby who appeared to be about the quads' age.

"This is my wife, Sophia, and our daughter, Andrea." Tate Graham smiled nervously at her. "And this is all the family I have, all in one room."

****

The babies stared at one another all through dinner. Andrea was completely overcome at the number of babies, and our babies was shocked to see another human their size.

Tate Graham explained that after graduation, and once he had a good job under his belt, he was gonna call Granny, but then he met Sophia, and felt like she was 'the one'. So he waited to make sure. She was, so they married. And just when he decided he could man up and show up, Sophia found out she was pregnant. It was a high risk pregnancy as Sophia was thirty-eight years old, so Tate Graham decided to wait for the outcome of that. They decided that Christmas time would be perfect, as Andrea would be old enough to travel easier, and here they was.

164

Sophia was from South Georgia and her accent was thick as molasses. We was mountain people, and our southern accents was very different than hers.

Sophia had just finished a tale about her own family, where they had spent Thanksgivin; when Lilly Ann raised her hand.

"You tawk funny, Sofa." Ah, my daughter, with so much room to talk.

Bensy tensed to speak, but Sophia shook her head slightly. "Oh, Sugah, I know! But I just cain't help it." Then she widened her eyes. "Are you gonna make fun of me?"

Lilly Ann shook her head violently. "No! Jesus would not wike that one wittle bit."

Sophia nodded. "That's right, Sugah, He wouldn't."

Sudden tears formed in Lilly Ann's eyes, much to our surprise. "The big kids make fun of the way I tawk sometimes when we are on the pwayground."

Well, that was the first we'd heard of it. We thought bein on the playground for fifteen minutes a day with the 'big kids' – that would be kindergarten and first grade – would be a harmless thing.

"What must your teacha say, Sugah?"

Lilly Ann dropped her head. "She don't know. I don't tewul on 'em."

"Do you want her to know?"

Lilly Ann shook her head again. "I just want dem to stop."

You could have heard a pin drop. Bensy took a deep, tearful breath. "Just be kind to them, Lilly Ann. They all need a lesson in kindness."

And, boy, I figured they would get one as soon as Bensy could talk to Lilly Ann's teacher.

I cleared my throat. "Well, Lilly Ann, maybe havin your new Aint Tate Graham and Uncle Sophia will cheer you up."

Everone at the table laughed.

"What?"

Bensy giggled. "I think you mean Aint Sophia and Uncle Tate Graham. You got it backwards, Charles."

At least it broke the tension.

"What do you think about that, Monte?" Granny asked.

Monte looked up from his mashed potatoes and blinked. "Huh?"

My boy is so sensitive.

The intro to his new aunt and uncle was repeated.

He nodded happily. "Unka Tate Gwaym and Aint Sopeeur."

Lilly Ann leaned in and confided. "Monte willy, *willy* cain't tawk pwain."

****

Christmas mornin come way too early for Bensy and me, but not for Lilly Ann. She drug Monte out of a deep slumber to see what was under the tree.

Everbody was happy, pictures was took, kids was dressed and off we went to Bensy's folks.

The food was great, and the gossip was stupendous because it was all about my family and we had been first hand witnesses to ever bit of it.

We dreaded takin down the tree when we got home, but there was no worries because the cats had done it for us. After scarin 'em half to death with the air horn, I reckon they decided revenge was in order the minute nobody was home to stop it.

Tears and shrieks from the two kids old enough to care withstandin, it was easier to get it out of the way.

Another Christmas had come and gone.

CHAPTER TWENTY-FOUR

We got our first big snow on New Year's Eve. Bensy's granny had come over for supper. When we started out the door to take her home after celebratin the New Year comin in, we was shocked to find about four or five inches on the ground and snow still comin down hard.

I figured if Lilly Ann and Monte had been allowed to stay up, Lilly Ann's snow radar would have kicked in, but us grownups didn't have a clue.

That's how it come to be that Bensy's Granny spent the night with us. Bensy loaned her a flannel gown and socks and we always have extra toothbrushes, so she was good to go.

The next mornin was pure chaos, what with the babies all needin to be tended to, Lilly Ann and Monte goin bonkers about wantin outside before daylight, nearly, and Granny Taylor spazzin out because she needed to get home. Why I don't know, as she lived alone.

Her only pet – if you could call him that – was Homer, the meanest tom cat that ever lived. He stayed under the porch and in the field out back. He only ate cat food at breakfast time. If you even looked at him, he'd growl and hiss and bunch up his fur like he was goin to eat you alive. Lemma had him a good warm bed under the porch, with a light bulb that burned 24/7 in the winter. It'd probably put him in a bad mood if I brung her home.

After breakfast, which is very similar to a world war at our house; Granny Taylor asked to use our phone. Bensy handed her the portable kitchen phone, and after wipin off the baby food that was on it, Granny Taylor disappeared to Lilly Ann's bedroom, where she'd spent the night.

We got busy cleanin up kitchen counters and babies so we could get outside and take pictures. Then we'd scoop up clean snow, make snow cream, eat it, wrap everbody up and have about ten minutes of fun. By then, somebody, probably Monte, would have to pee.

Just as we started out the door for clean snow, Granny Taylor come back into the kitchen. "This telephone went dead as a door nail. I reckon Agnes talked it to death."

Bensy laughed. "I forgot to put it back in the holder last night. I can charge it back up." She took the phone.

Granny Taylor shook her head. "You don't know Agnes. If that woman ain't got nuthin to say, she'll keep talkin till she thinks of somethin." She shrugged. "I reckon it's because of that confounded man of her'n. Bad nerves makin her chatter like a magpie all the live long day. Cain't see why in the world she married him. 'Course, hit's been sixty years ago, but I don't think he's much diff'ernt. 'Cept uglier, maybe."

"Granny, them's pretty harsh words. Is he that unlikable?" I asked.

"Well, I ain't never met nobody'd as want him as a pet."

I decided to leave it at that and get busy with my snow business.

Of all the pictures I took that day, the funniest one is of Granny Taylor, posin with the kids and Bensy. She looks put out, holdin the phone in one hand and a baby in the other. The phone is headed for her ear.

It wadn't till late afternoon that the snow melted enough I could take Granny Taylor home. By then she'd run the battery down on our other portable phone, and was workin on the first one again.

I don't know how that woman kept house, or had time to feed herself, for that matter.

And speakin of phones, my granny called about thirty minutes after I got home.

"Well," she started out. "I heard Lemmer spent the night with ya'll."

"Yep." I tried to sound cheerful, as Granny sounded mean. "Lemma didn't mean to spend the night, she got snowed in. Had to sleep with Lilly Ann, which means she probably didn't get much sleep."

"I reckon she done called everbody in the county to tell 'em she was thar. She was just braggin. Tryin to slight me's, what she was adoin."

"Now, Granny, I thought you and Lemma was good

friends."

"We are. But when it comes to fam'ly time, it's always a competition with her. Lord knows why, I shore don't."

I sighed. "Granny, do you want to spend the night with us tonight? Lilly Ann would be thrilled to share her bed again. Though let me remind you, she kicks like a mule."

There was a moment of silence. "I'll think about it." And she slammed down the phone.

Lord!

****

The next day we got a call from Dow Rutherford sayin the movie was ready for us to view. He'd already arranged with the local theatre to set up there for a private viewin the next Friday night. He told us when the movie was ready for a pre-premiere viewin, we would have a showin there again for whoever we wanted to invite. But for this night, we might even see scenes that wouldn't make the final cut.

Bensy started makin a list for the pre-premiere viewin. She might as well have just got the census and give that to Dow. I only hoped the theatre would hold everbody she was askin.

So a few evenins later, Bensy and me and our families sat in a otherwise empty theatre with Dow.

Wincy kept the babies and Monte at home. We bribed Lilly Ann and promised her if she got bored and was still good anyway, we'd buy her a surprise afterwards. And if she didn't behave, she'd get a surprise afterward, too, but she wouldn't like it. At all.

I admit it was pretty incredible seein our babies up there on a big screen. I could tell them apart (most the time), and of course, Bensy knowed ever time, except one. It was a scene where the family was gettin ready to go out, and the baby had on a cap. Bensy turned to me, horror on her face. "I don't know which one it is!" The fam'ly around us erupted into laughter.

Paula, Lilly Ann and Monte had a bit part in a crowd scene. They was the children of some actors who had a small speakin part. When Lilly Ann saw herself, she said, "Hoe-wee cow! Dar I am, Mama!"

I was right proud of Monte. He looked like an adorable angel, and didn't grab hisself even one time.

Wincy had the babies and Monte asleep by the time we got home. Lilly Ann had fell asleep in the car and barely woke up when Bensy got her in bed.

Wincy left after askin twenty questions, and Bensy and me went to bed shortly thereafter.

It was a sweet day.

****

We had invited Mara and Ron over for supper the followin

weekend.

Melissa was a little over two months old, and Bensy figured it was time for Mara to get out of the house.

We decided to throw caution to the wind and invite Tate Graham and Sophia over, too.

Because of his age, Tate Graham felt more like a cousin to me than an uncle. And since their baby, Andrea, was, well, a baby, we thought everone would fit in nicely and we could have a good time.

We locked the cats and dog out on the screen porch. They had a big box with an old blanket to curl up in and we'd even drug Dancer's dog house onto the porch. But of course, they chose to sit at the French door and watch us with pitiful expressions on their faces. I knowed a dog could do it, but the cats had it down pat, too.

Ron and Mara arrived first. I was suspicious because the twins was quiet and shy-like. Ron shrugged, swore they hadn't drugged them, that they was goin through some stage. Melissa was one of the prettiest babies I ever seen.

As they unbundled everbody, Tate Graham and his crew arrived.

Granny had already give Andrea a bunch of 'play purties' while they'd been here; one of which she grasped in her hand. It was a tiny pink bunny with a polka dot dress on.

Their presence had taken ten years off Granny's age, at least looks wise.

Introductions was made. Babies stared at other babies. The twins thawed out enough to be led into the livin room by Lilly Ann and Monte where they was watchin their 'Veggie Tales' movie.

Ron raked his mess of red hair till it was standin on end. I wondered if he ever combed the stuff. "I'm starvin. Ain't had time for nothin but a slam sammich for dinner."

Sophia grinned. "I think I know, but I must ask anyway. What in the world is a '*slam sammich*'?" Everthing she said was drawed out so, that sammich come out 'sa-am-mich'.

"Ah, it's whar you take two pieces of loaf bread, spread some Blue Plate across it and slam it together. Didn't even have a co-cola to wash it down with." He patted his large belly. "It's been a sad afternoon."

"Gee, Ron, I hope you had time for breakfast," I deadpanned.

"Oh, yeah. I had-" and he proceeded to tell us, but I ain't got room here to list it all.

Everbody laughed, except Mara. She just shook her head and walked into the kitchen. Sophia followed her.

That left us men with six babies between us, and four more under the age of five.

God help us.

The meal actually was real good. We drug two baby beds to the dinin room door and sat babies in them.

Melissa had just been fed, and she slept contentedly in her pack and play.

We got the kids' table situated, and Lilly Ann made sure all three boys behaved.

She's gonna make a great wife someday.

We all told stories and laughed a lot.

After the table was cleared and the dishwasher filled, we was able to visit just a little longer before the kids all started unravelin.

Ron and Mara called it a night. We loaded up a twin in each arm for Ron and the baby for Mara.

Tate Graham asked if they could stay a little longer, and we said of course. I had a funny feelin all night that he'd wanted to say somethin to me, so I figured I was about to find out what that was.

All the babies was asleep, piled up like puppies. Lilly Ann and Monte was fadin fast. I knowed it was goin to make later on tonight harder, as we had to get them to bed properly and hope no one woke up fully, but it seemed like a small price to pay, in hindsight.

Tate Graham said, "Mama's not wantin us to leave, but school starts back and I have to get back to class, so we'll be leavin tomorrow afternoon." He fiddled with his glass, but finally said, "Did you know the land next to you is for sale?"

"Has Lavish and Gabby come down on the price?" Lavish and Gabby Gibson had farmed that land for forty years. It had lain fallow for twenty. They was both nearin ninety. They'd outlived both their children. They had two grandchildren, and I guessed they was wantin to leave them money, as they was both raised city and probably not interested in a farm. "I priced it, then tried to forget. I've just been prayin no contractor would pick it up and put three or four dozen cookie cutter houses on it."

Tate Graham nodded. "Mama told me about it. Made Sophia and me think...if I could get a teachin job close by, what if we bought the land? We could put a trailer on it till we could get a house built or remodel the Gibson house, if it's worth savin." He leaned forward, lookin me straight in the eye. "But all that would be contingent on if you would consider goin bigger in the cattle business and we could partner."

"How big?" I asked. I felt my heart rate speed up.

Tate Graham grinned. "Well I was thinkin you could become a gentleman farmer slash rancher. I don't want to give up teachin. For all I know, you don't want to give up your job, either." He glanced at Sophia, and she nodded slightly. "When Sophia's grandfather died, she was left a great deal of money. She's the eldest grandchild and the amount is substantial. We would love to use some of it like this."

Sophia smiled. "Since we've been here, I've fallen in love with all of you. And to be able to raise our child next door with cousins her age, and for me to have ya'll and your family. Well. It seems like a dream come true. Don't get me wrong, I love my family, but there's no one close to my age, or Andrea's age." Tears glistened in her eyes. "This would be a privilege, if you think it's somethin you might want."

I looked over at Bensy and she looked as thunder struck as I felt.

"I don't know what to say, Tate Graham. I reckon Bensy and me will have to pray hard talk some and think about it. But I will say, it sounds awful good." I shook my head. "Are you sayin I could quit my job and concentrate on havin a lot of cattle, maybe expand farmin, too?"

"That's exactly what I'm sayin. I really don't want to give up teachin. I found somethin after all these years that I'm good at. I make a difference. It's my passion, I guess. But this is a dream for me, too. To come back home; to have somethin to tie me to family."

I nodded. "I can understand that."

He slapped his hands on his legs. "Well, we've given you somethin to think about and now we need to get out of here so everybody can get a good night's sleep."

Shortly after that, they left to go back to sleep at Granny's.

Stunned, I asked myself: Could this be a dream come true for us too?

CHAPTER TWENTY-FIVE

Fact is, Bensy and me hardly got sleep at all that night. We started off with prayer, and then commenced to talk. How much would it take for us to live – really live –farmin and havin cattle?

We finally decided. If Tate Graham and Sophia was serious, we'd take them up on it, if he thought I could make enough what with still workin a couple of days a week.

But before I talked to them, Bensy and me agreed the person I really needed to talk to about it was Ron. He knowed all about farmin and workin.

****

Ron and me got to meet up for breakfast on Saturday mornin. When we finally had our food under our belts (well, it was more like *over* Ron's belt), we settled back in the booth and I spilled everthing that Tate Graham had offered.

"Dang it Charles, have you scoped it out any?"

"Tate Graham sent me a detailed e-mail. He wants three acres private for his house, yard, studio, stuff like that." I changed the subject slightly for a moment. "Turns out Tate Graham thinks he's got a book in him. They are gonna build a small guest house for when Sophia's family visits. But mostly he's gonna use it for an office to get his novel off the ground."

Ron just stared at me, so I got back to the subject at hand. "Okay, so anyway, the rest of the land, which they are payin for *in cash* will be used for mostly cattle, with some acreage saved for fruit trees and growin whatever food I want. I ain't researched any of that yet. Haven't had time. We split profits 40/50 until he's made enough to pay back half of what it cost him, because he feels like his wife should have that back, although she disagrees. Then it's 50/50. Now, I disagree with this – he's put all his money and all I'll do is give up my job when I can and do the work."

"You disagree," Ron said, "Because you ain't got a clue as to what work means when it comes to somethin like this. Ya'll will have to hire folks in, pretty close to right off the bat. You'll be purchasin more cattle, plantin trees and plants *after* you get the land ready. Puttin up fencin. Lord!" He did the thing with his hair. "Makes me tired to think about it all."

I felt my heart sink. "What you're sayin is they ain't gonna be no profit for a long time."

"Depends on how savvy you are with the cattle. Problem is, I don't know how you can work at your job and do this. And I don't know how you can do this without money. You talked to Roscoe yet?"

Roscoe was the head boss. "No. I hope he'll let me cut down to three days a week for a while." I slumped back in my seat. "But I can't do that without money to compensate. We are barely scrapin by as it is. In fact, we wouldn't be scrapin by if it wadn't for the whole town helpin us and the movie thing. I had high hopes of puttin any money the quads was paid into a savins account, but we're havin to use it to keep them fed and clothed."

"Well, it's an incredible opportunity."

"Bensy and me stayed up half of a night lookin at our finances. What we need to make ends meet is about two hundred and fifty dollars a month more than I'm makin right now."

Ron grinned. "Yet-"

"Yet we haven't missed payin a bill. God is slippin money into our account, I reckon."

"I know ya'll have prayed about it. God can do the impossible, that's what He does best."

"What would you do?"

"If Mara said okay, I'd jump in with both feet." He shrugged. "But I love cattle and farmin. I wish I could do that all the time instead of work at a payin job, too. *You* have to want that, too, or it won't work."

"I was hopin maybe I could do both for a while."

"I don't see how, buddy. The size of what you're describin is gonna take all your time and others, too. And I mean *all* your time."

I left feelin worse that when I'd got there. But I didn't know how to say no, either.

I come into the house with a long face, but Bensy met me at the door with a smile. "Come look!" she whispered.

I tiptoed into the livin room. All the quads was in the floor. They was grabbin the couch and pullin up, wobblin to a stand. They was squealin at each other. Then Paula dropped down and got on all fours, tryin to figure out the crawlin thing.

"Wow." I turned to Bensy, grinnin like a fool. "When did this start?"

"About five minutes before you drove up. Lilly Ann and Monte was helpin at first, but as soon as the babies got the knack of it, they went back to their toys."

I walked on in and sat down on the couch. "Look at you!" I said, as they grinned up at me. John Mark grabbed my pants leg and pulled up.

"Dah!" he proclaimed.

Suddenly, everthing was right with the world.

****

Bensy was adamant that if that's what my desire was, to call Tate Graham and tell him. But I had to lay our financial troubles out real clear, and be honest about what Ron had said about needin others to work.

So, I did.

Tate Graham laughed. "Man, Charles, I already knew that. I guess I thought you understood. I know you have to have a salary. It's pretty obvious Bensy can't go to work. We have to get together in person. You are goin to be paid. We are goin to hire a consultant who will put together exactly how many workers we need. Someone who will be able to give a close estimate of costs regardin cattle, seed, plants, trees, gettin the land ready." He paused. "I've done a lot of research myself. It won't be cheap. But once we get it started up, we should do fine. So when I'm old enough to retire, I can live easy."

"Tate Graham, your wife is rich, ain't she?"

"Yep. Very."

"Oh. I guess I didn't realize she was *rich*, rich." I took a deep breath. "Okay. Let's make a date to get together with your consultant and start plannin. I'm in."

"Praise the Lord!" Tate Graham hollered.

Well, that was new. I felt a burden lift plumb off my shoulders.

CHAPTER TWENTY-SIX

Ah, Valentine's. A man's worst enemy.

But this year, I figured I had it whipped.

First off, Wincy and Ham was pickin up all the kids and they was spendin the night with them. I made sure they wadn't goin to jump out of a second story window or somethin, but Wincy assured me her niece, who was fifteen, was comin, too, and Ham was as excited as she.

I bet he wouldn't be excited for long. Probably would take a vow of celibacy.

Anyway, Mama and Daddy had give me a fifty dollar gift certificate to the fancy restaurant we loved, so that was covered. And I went to the florist and she put me together a sweet little bouquet of pink and white flowers that didn't break the bank. I stopped by the bakery and bought Bensy a big brownie, and they put it in a pink sack with a white ribbon on it, so it looked like a million dollars.

I was a man on the right track.

Plus, the night looked promisin, if you know what I mean. No babies wakin up. No Monte comin in to report on his potty adventures. No Lilly Ann to come in and complain about her bed bein too hot/cold.

We could shut the bedroom door and keep the four leggeds out, at least for a little while.

Life looked good.

And, it was. It was. The flowers and brownie was a hit. The restaurant food was wonderful, the empty house was sweet and we pretended we was newlyweds.

We cuddled up to sleep like spoons.

Then the phone rang.

All four of the babies was runnin a fever and Monte was throwin up. Lilly Ann was cryin because she was afraid she *might* throw up.

And, actually, Ham said, nobody else felt too good either.

The end of Valentine's was a lot more excitin than the beginnin.

At least Cupid got to shoot his arrow.

****

The next four days was spent at the pediatrician, drugstore, and laundry room. Not necessarily in that order.

Of course, Bensy and me come down with it as soon as the kids got over it. Our mamas had to come and get the kids, and Wincy come to see about us and help, as she figured she couldn't get it again and didn't want our grannies exposed.

I agreed. This woulda killed a lesser man.

Bensy rolled her eyes and hit me in the shoulder when I said that, bein as she was sicker than me.

Finally, I got better after two days and went back to work. Bensy's lingered a bit more, but soon she was up and about.

Life returned to normal, and I prepared to meet with Tate Graham and the consultant.

I looked pretty good, too. Lost four pounds with the virus.

I didn't understand a lot of what was said about gradual growth, and all the charts he had. I did understand when he talked about cattle cost, because Ron had educated me.

In fact, Tate Graham was interested in seein if Ron would work with us at the beginnin as a consultant while purchasin more cattle to go with my cows.

I come home and talked to Roscoe. I would begin workin three days a week startin next month, which was March, and slowly work my way into bein unemployed by him. He congratulated me, and said if things didn't work out, I'd always have some kind of job with him. That made me feel safer than I had through the whole deal.

Then I called Ron, who was happier than a dead pig in slop. I told him what Tate Graham was payin by the hour, and he nearly cried with joy.

This was gettin better and better.

****

In my life, there ain't never been much time to sit and contemplate how worried I might be about somethin. With family and work, plus Dow callin to say he'd set up a date for the movie to show, I reckon I just sailed right along.

Dow explained this was the finished product, and they was doin what they called test audiences. Of course, we was the first test audience. I laughed and said 'like nobody here would dislike it', and he laughed, too. I guess that's cheatin a little, havin it here, but on the other hand, it did seem only fair to us.

He said it would be a year or so before it actually come out in all the theatres. I figured by then, everbody here would go back to see it, and I bet he figured the same thing.

Bensy got on the horn and started callin folks, and Dow extended personal invitations to just about everbody in the county. The owner of the movie theatre begin puttin posters up all over town, and even bought a few spots on the radio.

Uncle Wend called, more excited than I'd ever heard him. "The wife and I are so pleased for ya'll about this. You know, we hardly go to the movies. I'm more of a reader myself. Actually you could say I'm omnilegent."

I reckon I could say that, but it was safer not to.

"Now, ya'll aren't goin to let Monte, er, little ones, come to the movie, are you?"

"No, Uncle Wend. They'd be too disruptive. We are gonna

find a sitter, I hope."

He sighed, relieved. "I'm not talkin bad about the boy, but you and I both know it would be rather disturbin. He has a way of becomin a rather polrumptious lad."

He was waitin on my reply. So I drug one up. "Uh-huh."

"He's just so young. He simply has a cacoethes for nonsensical behavior, but I'm sure it's his age."

"I'm sure." I was beginnin to get a headache.

Uncle Wend cleared his throat. "Well, I must be goin now. Your Aunt Marveena wants to shop for somethin new to wear to this event." He lowered his voice to a near whisper. "She is sorely afflicted with Onionmania, you know. I must never let her go near a mall alone."

"Um, well. I'm sorry to hear that, Uncle Wend." I truly was, whatever it meant.

"I'm sure we'll be talkin soon."

"You betcha."

And he hung up.

I went to the computer to look up what the heck was wrong with Aunt Marveena.

****

Do you know how impossible it was to try and find a baby

sitter that night? They wadn't nobody what wanted to stay home with a bunch of babies and not see the movie. Us gettin to see the movie several months before the rest of the country was the talk of the town.

Dow laughed when we told him we couldn't find a babysitter. He said he'd already figured that one out. He'd rigged it up so the movie would be showin on a big screen TV in the church nursery. Anybody who had kids under six could bring them there and professional childcare from his personal stable (he said that, not me) would take care of the kids, feedin them and playin with them. Anyone who wanted to stay with their kids could see the movie on the big screen. He'd set that up especially for Lilly Ann and Monte.

That night, Lilly Ann pitched a fit because she wadn't goin with us. But Bensy is such a good mama. She sat Miss Priss down and told her how much trouble Dow had gone to, to make a special movie house for kids so they could have snacks and move around if they needed to. She told her about the people who would be makin them food and playin games too, if they didn't want to see the movie. The topper was this: Bensy told Lilly Ann no one would be allowed to speak or have food in the big theatre.

Lilly Ann's eyes widened. "Why fowevah not?" she asked.

"Because there will be important boss people there to make sure Dow is doin a good job. If people talk or eat, they will think people aren't payin attention because the movie isn't good."

Lilly Ann was gettin steamed. "Dow is a wuv-wee man. Dey bedder not do nuffin bad to him."

Bensy nodded. "That's right. So me and your daddy have to be on our best behavior." Bensy stood up and started helpin Lilly Ann with her coat. "Now, you be sure and thank Dow for everthing he's done for the kids – especially you and Monte – he knowed you'd want to see the movie first thing!"

"Oh, I will, Mama. I surewee won't forget."

"That's my girl!"

By the time this conversation had ended, I had all the babies strapped in and Monte too. "We're ready to go!" I hollered from the front door, keepin an eye on the van full of baby cargo. "Come on!"

"We are comin, Daddy. Keep your coat on!" Lilly Ann hollered back as she barreled toward the front door. I scooped her up and hauled her to the van; causin Lilly Ann to giggle all the way.

Bensy locked the door, got in, and off we went to the biggest event this town had seen in years.

Town was a madhouse. People had parked as far away as the Methodist church, which was on the other side of town, and walked. All the parents that had left their kids at the First

Baptist Church nursery had parked there or around there, and walked. The town square was completely full, the library's parkin lot was full. All the stores who had 'reserved for customer only' parkin spots was filled, too, but I didn't imagine there'd be any hard feelins over it tonight.

Our grannies and parents was both there, as was Tate Graham and Sophia. Everone was dressed in nice clothes, but of course Uncle Wend and Aunt Marveena looked like they was goin on the red carpet in Hollywood. I'da been embarrassed, but no one would have expected less of Uncle Wend. Granny called him a fool under her breath, and I could have sworn I heard Mama whisper to Granny, "Well, at least he ain't got on four pair of drawers." And Granny slapped at her.

I needed to remember to ask what the heck that was about later.

Ron and Mara was grinnin from ear to ear, and Ron slapped me on the back so hard I nearly fell. It don't pay to get a big feller like him excited or proud of you.

The Parker twins was handin out tickets for a big sale they was havin the next day, and somebody was gonna win fifty dollars if they had the right ticket. All they had to do was show up.

Sammy walked up to me, grinnin sheepishly, to ask how Dancer was doin. I looked at him and deadpanned. "She's fine. We are starvin to death, but she's fine."

He grinned and kept on goin.

Wincy and Ham told us they couldn't believe they was hobnobbin with grownups tonight, with not a person in sight who looked like they needed their mama.

Lloyd and Lisa Singleton showed up. They'd moved to Alabama a few months ago, and it sure was good to see them. Lisa said she was beginnin to like where they lived, and Lloyd asked me if I wanted to go skinny dippin. I asked him where his Aunt Vernall was.

Mabel showed up by herself. Said weren't no doctor comin that she knowed of, but she imagined I'd seen enough of them anyhow, and I opined that was hittin it pretty close.

But, actually, I think I did see Dr. Spratin there. He's such a big man, he's hard to miss, but I didn't bother to hunt him down to speak. He'd just analyze why I'd gone to the bother.

Chigger Lloyd was there and was talkin about how he loved this time of year, bein itch free and all. Bless his heart.

I reckon just about everbody we have ever known was right there. My boss (who was about to be my ex-boss) come and wished me well just as we all filed into the theatre.

It was packed. They even filled up the old balcony and let ten people into the projector's office.

They let twenty-five people stand in the lobby, for there was a big screen TV out there.

Dow called, and the nursery at First Baptist said they could take a dozen adults to watch it on the big screen, so some people scurried there.

And not everbody got in.

Dow was astonished. He made a call to some technician, who said they could splice the feed and put another big screen TV up in the sanctuary of the church if we could all wait about thirty minutes.

All applauded 'yes', so the town had a gossip fest while people got settled in at the church.

This was a prime opportunity. I leaned over to Mama and asked, "What was you sayin to Granny about havin on four pair of panties?"

Mama rolled her eyes. "I took her to the doctor yesterday to have her blood work done and she told me as we was walkin in that she had on four pair of drawers. When I asked why in the thunder did she do that, she said her rear end had sagged so bad her britches looked empty. She thought addin a little paddin would help. There ain't no tellin what the doctor thought when he had to pull down four pair of bloomers to palpitate her belly. I refused to go in there with her."

I laughed and sat back, winkin at Bensy. That was our sign, so she now knowed I had a good tale for her when we got home.

I reckon the movie was a success. I heard people laugh, sniff tears back and cheer when one of our babies showed up. They gave it a standin ovation and our backs was patted near to death.

By the time we got home and got everbody in bed, my eyes was crossed with fatigue.

I did remember to share Granny's four drawers moment with Bensy, though. She went to sleep with a smile on her face.

CHAPTER TWENTY-SEVEN

The next mornin Mike Crenshaw, our mayor, called. Mike is a fairly young fella who was voted in by a huge percentage when our old mayor threw in the towel and retired. Mike was all excited about the movie and wanted to know if Bensy, me, and the kids would be the lead in the Easter parade.

He said the Easter Bunny would be right behind us, and each of the kids could get a free photo with him.

The parade was always on Saturday mornin, followed by a Easter Egg hunt, then a county wide cookout at the park with a live band in the gazebo. Their music ranged from *"He Arose!"* to *"In Your Easter Bonnet"*.

I told Mike to hang on a minute and went to find Bensy, who was in the laundry room buried under dirty clothes. She said "Sure why not" like I was askin her if she wanted pizza for supper.

You get used to fame, I reckon.

I told Mike yes and went to write it down on the calendar. Since Easter was early this year, in March, I figured we needed to buy warm outfits for everone.

As I was tryin to figure out how we could afford that plus Easter outfits for Sunday mornin, Bensy come in the livin room with the same thing on her mind.

"I'll go to the thrift store and see if I can find anything. You'd be surprised at the cute stuff for kids. They outgrow clothes so fast they still look like new."

"I bet you cain't find matchin outfits for the quads."

"They are good for the parade. I've got yellow jackets, white t-shirts and blue jeans, that's good enough for how cold it will be. Lilly Ann will need a brighter jacket and Monte needs new stuff anyhow. He's outgrowin everthing he's got."

That was the truth. He had hit a growth spurt that even surprised my mama when she went three days without seein him. We measured him and he'd grown an inch in those three days.

We was used to the quads growin in leaps and bounds; after all, they'd be a year old next month.

Lilly Ann was sort of stable in growth at the moment, givin us a financial break.

When Bensy got back from the thrift store, she had a sack full and had spent less than forty dollars.

I love my wife.

She'd actually found matchin Easter dresses for Lilly Ann and Paula. Monte would look spiffy in his dress pants, shirt and little bowtie, which he immediately wanted to put on. We let him wear it for about five minutes, then convinced him it had to be perfect for Easter.

The other three boys had sort of matchin long sleeve shirts and pants. Good enough, anyway.

She even found a practically brand new light blue shirt for me, which would go great with my navy blazer.

That was it. I looked at her. "Where's your new outfit?"

She blushed a little. "I don't need anything new. I've got a outfit I couldn't get in right after Monte, but now I finally can wear it."

She could tell I was about to protest when she stopped me. "I mean it, Charles. I'm not bein the 'poor little old me' wife. I really do want to wear the dress and show off my figure." She looked up at me. "Is that bein too vain for Easter?"

I grinned and hugged her up. "No, ma'am, it ain't. I think you should be pleased with yourself about how purty you are."

Everthing was hung up carefully and we really did have pizza for supper.

****

We went to Good Friday services that evenin. It was 42 degrees and fallin. They was some worried expressions on faces about the parade, but the pastor reminded everone we was there to be in awe of what was done for us by the Lord, not worry about a parade. I had to agree. We was all bundled up, and with Mama's help, we spread out on one pew and was together for the service. It was a short service, one song by a soloist, communion, a short lesson on where we was in history on the first Good Friday and readin of scripture that stopped when Jesus was laid in the tomb.

It was soberin lesson, so solemn that the kids picked up on it all and was quiet.

Saturday mornin it was 34 degrees when we got up. Mike called to make sure we was up to a very cold parade. I told him we was dressin in layers, and as long as it stayed above freezin, we wadn't too worried.

The cold didn't keep people away. The entire town seemed to be lined up, that is if they wadn't part of the parade. Of course, the high school band played, and the football players and cheerleaders was there. The cheerleaders was in sweat pants and sweat shirts, they wadn't stupid. The Easter Bunny, who skipped around right behind us, threw out plastic Easter eggs with candy in them.

And I'll be a monkey's uncle if it didn't start snowin about a block into the parade.

This seemed to make everone giddy, even the adults.

When we got back around full circle, they had barrels burnin for heat, and the Methodists was givin away hot chocolate. Parents was standin in line with their younguns for photo ops with the Easter Bunny.

The pictures turned out really good, what with the snow comin down all around.

We got one picture with Lilly Ann holdin Paula; Monte on his knees holdin Matthew steady, and the Easter Bunny with the other two; one in each paw. The snow was fallin pretty heavy and everone had the giggles.

Well, except the Easter Bunny. His face sorta was frozen in place, if you know what I mean.

By lunch time the snow was gone and it was in the forties. Kids stayed pretty warm rompin around, playin. The band was lively, and a lot of the people sang along with many of the songs.

By the middle of the afternoon the kids was droopin and the adults certainly was.

I'd never been so glad to walk in my front door and feel glorious heated air.

****

Easter mornin always made me feel giddy. First it's the kids seein what the Easter Bunny brung them...usually we allowed one stuffed animal each and Bensy always made a dozen 'real' Easter eggs for them to hide on Sunday afternoon (and that year Lilly Ann was finally old enough that she got to help). But the real feelins of elation was when we got to church. Almost everone was dressed up more than usual, there was twice as many folks there as usual, and we greeted one another with "He is Risen!" which gave me goose bumps.

After church, we all gathered at Bensy's Granny Taylor's and had ham and potato salad and who knows what else. We went home, we napped, and then we hid eggs. Lilly Ann and Monte had a blast.

Just like I did.

By Sunday night we was all pretty tired. My little Easter parade stars was tuckered out.

When we got them settled in, we collapsed on the couch.

"The preacher said you sure looked pretty today. He said you was glowin. If he wadn't the preacher, I'da got jealous."

Bensy poked my arm. "I appreciate the comment. A few other people bragged on me, too. I think it's cause I've lost all my baby fat and I really love that dress I wore."

"Maybe it's because you're a beautiful woman, Bensy Taylor Simpson." I reached over and kissed her. "I'm not sure you realize that all the time."

She laughed. "Thank you, sir. Better watch your mouth or it could get you in some trouble."

I waggled my eyebrows. "That's the kind of trouble I like."

"You're a good man, Charlie Brown."

"I hate bein called Charlie."

She giggled. We snuggled.

Life was good.

CHAPTER TWENTY-EIGHT

Spring was nearly here. The quads was all tryin to walk, except for John Mark. He'd pull up on the couch or a chair (or your leg) and worriedly watch the others as they would step, fall, get up, step, fall and give up and crawl to their destination. If he turned loose of whatever he was holdin onto, he simply sat down on his bottom and crawled off.

The cats was stayin way out of the way, fearful they was goin to get set on. Dancer went from one baby to the other, tryin to make sure they was all okay. She didn't like them fallin down. Lilly Ann laughed, Monte tried to chase whichever one was attemptin to walk, holdin a pillow close to their bottom so they'd land on it, which of course, they never did.

Uncle Wend come by one evenin, lookin frazzled. I'd never seen him look quite so disheveled.

"I had to go somewhere besides home. I don't want to upset Marveena. But that fool Brownlow McGee is at it again. You know he is usually quite loquacious; but this evenin, he was behavin in a prevaricate manner." Uncle Wend began to pace a bit back and forth. "Oh, he thought he was bein duplicitous, but it takes more than what he has to offer to fool me! He's nothin but a blaltaroon!" He shook his fist in the air. "He should stop fudgellin and do some real work!" He was beginnin to look wild eyed. "He's nothin but a quomodocunquizin smatchet!"

I stuck my finger in my ear to make sure it wadn't bleedin. "Sounds like you'd welcome him bout like you'd welcome a ornery skunk trapped under your front porch." He nodded vigorously. "So, um, what exactly is he accusin you of?"

"He doesn't think I am qualified to run for city council. He wants that ersatz Coatus Picklesimmer to run." He shook his head. "You know Coatus has always been a solivagant. Why, add that to his tendency toward endless rodomontades about hisself, and I don't think he's trustworthy."

No joke.

Uncle Wend suddenly sat down, hard, on the couch. I jumped. "Sorry, my boy. Feelin a bit zwodder, after all that rantin."

Was that bad? Was that good? "Can I get you anything?"

"No, no. Well, perhaps a glass of water."

"Sure thing."

As I started out of the room, he added, "And a cookie or two, if you have any."

"I'll check."

Bensy met me in the kitchen. "I looked up zwodder. Don't worry, it just means sleepy," She whispered.

"After the way he's been goin on, I was afraid it met 'stroke-like'," I whispered back.

She grinned and reached for two Oreos, put them in a napkin and ushered me out of the kitchen with them and the water.

A half hour later, after commentin that our cats was lagopodous, he left.

I closed the door behind him.

And locked it.

****

Spring had us hoppin like a six-legged toad frog. What with cattle comin in after the pasture had been secured, and new chicken houses built and chickens comin in, and ground bein plowed to prepare a large garden, it was almost sleeplessness for Tate Graham. He was tryin to get his family moved into a trailer in between drivin back and forth most nights from teachin his last year there. He'd done interviewed and got hisself a job here, startin in the fall; which give him the whole summer to help me get this circus goin.

We'd decided the garden this year would only be big enough for our families to eat out of and maybe can a little.

By next year we hoped to expand in order to sell to farmers' markets within a hundred-mile radius.

That mornin, Paula had waked up from her nap while the others was still sleepin, so I picked her up and off we went to walk over and see what all was goin on.

Tate Graham was already there, sweatin like he'd been at it for a while.

"Good Saturday mornin to you, Nephew," he said. He reached out and shook Paula's hand, which she snatched back and held to her chest, givin him a mean Taylor look, if I'd ever seen one.

Tate Graham shook his head. "Moody women."

"Just woke up from her mornin nap. And her mama is a Taylor."

"Don't I know it." Tate Graham grinned. He turned, lookin out over the pasture. "Well, Charles, what do you think of the herd?"

Cows was grazin all around. I was propped up on one side of the fence, Tate Graham on the other.

"Prettiest bunch of cows I ever seen. Glad we could get some more of what I done had. I think it's a very good start."

Tate Graham nodded. "Me too. Maybe by fall we can invest in a good bull. But I want us to take our time and look for a really good pedigreed one. Lot of money can be made."

One of the cows started saunterin over to us. Paula's eyes got really big. "Moo!" she hollered.

"Did you hear that? She said a new word! She said moo!"

Tate Graham laughed. "She surely did." He took a deep breath and mooed real loud.

Paula giggled and the cow hurried forward as though he'd said somethin of utmost importance.

But then Tate Graham's cell phone rang, and suddenly he was "Yes, sir. I'm really lookin forward to it."

I waved, Paula waved, mutterin, "Bye, bye, Moo." Tate Graham waved back.

As soon as I got back to the house, I sat Paula down and rushed into the kitchen where Bensy and Lilly Ann was fixin cereal for the now awake tribe. "Guess what! Paula saw a cow and said moo!"

Lilly Ann rolled her eyes. "Of course she did, Daddy. I been learnin her with dis." She jumped off her stool and ran out, comin right back with a large picture of a cow.

Paula took one look, pointed and hollered, "Moo!"

"Well," I said, deflated, "She recognized a real one, too."

Bensy grinned. "They are all really smart, aren't they?"

That's what I wanted to hear all along. "Yes, I think they are. Takes after you, of course."

She laughed – or smirked – "Of course they do."

After everone had their cereal and temporarily occupied by one thing or another, Bensy and I sat at the kitchen table for a few precious moments of grown up conversation.

We talked about the cattle and chicken houses and Tate Graham and Sophia's move.

"You know Bud and Suzie are tryin to help sell Tate Graham's house. They don't live too far away. Bud said they'd be glad to keep a watch on it, be there when the realtor shows up, that kind of thing." Bud was my late granddaddy's brother, and Suzi, his wife of forever.

I vaguely remembered this. Sophia or Tate Graham one had mentioned it briefly one evenin when we was porch settin with coffee. Said somethin about what a relief it would be not to have to run over there all the time.

I nodded. "Right nice of them. It has to be bothersome if you got other plans and have to go over there while they show the house."

Bensy giggled. "Well, the realtor was tellin Suzi what a nice job the company was doin and how Suzi didn't need to worry. Talked to her about all the extras they was doin, and mentioned they would even have a aerial shot of the house to show folks. Well, since she told Suzi about that, ever time she's heard a airplane, she's sent Bud over to make sure the cushions on the patio furniture was straight and that the garage door was shut and such."

I grinned. "Dudn't somebody need to tell Aint Suzi about google map?"

Bensy said, "I thought about it…but Bud's gettin purdy fat. I think the exercise will do him good."

Then I brought up the garden. "This year it's just gonna be big enough for all our families to have fresh vegetables. And you womenfolk can do some cannin, too, I reckon."

Bensy looked at me like I had two heads. "And just how am I gonna do that, Charles Simpson, with six children under the age of six? Do you realize the quads will be two this time next year? May I remind you that Monte has just turned three and it's not much better yet?"

I paled. I'd never thought that far. How could any house survive four two year olds, three of them boys. We was doomed.

Bensy looked closely at me. "Charles, you're pale."

I squinted at her. "So are you. Come to think of it, I've noticed that about you lately."

She sighed and come over and sat down in my lap. "I think a large garden is a great idea. Cookin fresh vegetables will be a big job, but I want my family to eat healthy. As long as we can afford Wincy still comin, I can manage. And maybe the next year, when the quads are three, I can think about cannin. But for now," she said, bumpin noses with me, "We palefaces have lots of little Injuns to take care of."

CHAPTER TWENTY-NINE

I think it was the prettiest spring I ever seen. Whatever bloomed was doin its finest to show off. Hens was broody, cows was pregnant by the best bull's sperm Tate Graham could buy.

I could almost see baby chicks and wobbly calves before my eyes.

The downside to spring was the quads all had some kind of allergy thing goin on and we was needin to invest in stock in tissue paper. I swan, I ain't never seen so much snot, if you'll pardon my French.

The remodelin of the old Gibson house was under way. Tate Graham said thankfully it was solid as a rock and just needed cosmetic work to go along with a new roof and plumbin, as well as a new sun room in the back that Sophia was all excited about. Apparently Lavish and Gabby had the place rewired some years ago when the house caught fire because of the old electrical system. There hadn't been much damage to the house, but scared them a right smart.

And, of course, the quads first birthday was comin up. The family had planned a pretty simple party, if havin a house full of one year olds and their siblins is your idea of simple.

The grannies had said they wanted to spend the money on decorations and cake makin, and whatever else it would cost. I told Granny I didn't want her spendin too much money, and she said, "Don't make no never mind about that, child. I cain't hardly wait to get it done."

But, then, of course, the whole town decided they needed to get involved, too. Before the mayor could start his yackin, I told him I'd talk to Bensy.

We discussed it, and felt like we ought to let it be done…but first, our family would celebrate in private.

Then I left a message on his voice mail and told him yes, to let me know about dates and such.

It was the best family get together I think we ever had. We'd also invited a few friends, of course, so they was plenty of chaos and mess.

Best party, ever.

So when the mayor called the second time and offered his congratulations on survivin the first year (and I was sure that'd be the first part of his speech, ha, ha.) He told us how proud he was to know us, and that the town was eager to celebrate the quads birthday. He wanted to rent the banquet hall next to the fire station (as if the party wouldn't be excitin enough), and that TV, newspaper, radio, as well as the Parker Brothers havin a professional takin photos and video, would all be coverin the event.

There would be door prizes provided by local businesses, games (guess which baby is which in a picture, if you get them all right you win $400.00, that kind of thing.) I asked him if Bensy could play the game, we could use an extra $400.00. He laughed and said, "No."

And speeches. He forgot to mention speeches.

So: The mayor spoke, the doctors spoke, both Dr. Smith who discovered a multiple birth pregnancy (and got the number wrong, but he failed to mention that) and Dr. Kettle who was the doctor for the high risk pregnancy, the Parker brothers spoke, our pastor nearly preached, and then the mayor took another turn.

He then asked for a speech from Bensy. I had been lulled into a false sense of security when Bensy turned to me and with a sugary voice and eyes of steel told me to go first.

I stuttered at first, but tried to talk about how unbelievable the past year had been to me, the true shock and awe of four tiny babies survivin and comin home to be a part of our family, the blessins that had come from it all, the old friends comin through for us, the new friends we had made because of the babies. I talked about all the help received from people we didn't even know, and how help still poured in, a year later.

I told them we could not have made it this far without the love that I felt, right then, right there, in that room.

I got a little teary eyed, and I saw Mama cryin a little, too.

Then I stepped down and motioned for Bensy to take the mic.

Bensy stood up. I thought how pretty she looked. Her hair was all fixed, make up done, that new dress she loved. Why, she was purely glowin.

Bensy started off by sayin she agreed with me about the past year, how amazin it had all been.

She said she was also so thankful to everone that she could never express how much it all had meant to her.

"But the most amazin thing that's happened to me this year happened to me just this mornin."

Now, I'd been with her all mornin, so I was tryin to figure out what she was goin to say. She was smilin, but her lips was tremblin a little. I looked around at her mama and granny, and they looked as mystified as I felt.

Then she glanced over at me, then Dr. Cutts, and my stomach dropped ten stories.

She had took a pregnancy test and it was positive.

Gasps filled the auditorium.

Then them little black specks started showin up in my eyes, just like I'd been knocked in the head on the playground.

Again.

CHAPTER THIRTY

How did this happen? I'd gone back and retested, just like they told me to. The doc had said I was good to go. So I figured nothin else was necessary. But seein the look on Mable and the doc's face at the party when Bensy made her announcement made me figure they'd forgot somethin.

Well, what went through my mind right then and there was if it was a boy we'd name it Mickey, after Dr. Cutts, and if it was a girl, we'd name it Mabel.

I sure hoped it wadn't a girl, in that case, cause Mabel was one of the orneriest people I ever knowed.

****

The next mornin, after a near sleepless night, we headed to our respective doctors. Dr. Cutts and Dr. Smith's offices was in the same medical buildin complex.

"Are you sure you don't want me to go with you?" I asked Bensy.

"No. It's just a blood test, mostly. You go on to see Dr. Cutts."

"I don't know whether to hit him or slap him with a law suit."

Bensy smiled. "Neither. What's meant to be, is meant to be. Buck up, Charles, it's just one more child."

I looked at her, knowin she was tryin to make me feel better, when it should be the other way 'round. But it'd always been that way, even when we was little kids.

"Okay. I promise no violence unless Mabel gets smart with me."

"Atta boy." We parked and got out. I gave Bensy a chaste peck on the cheek before goin my way.

"If I was you, that's all I'd ever do for the rest of my life." I turned to see which smart aleck was speakin to me.

"Ain't that the truth?" I said. "But I'm a weak man and love my wife."

Ron shook his head. "I'm beggin you to not go in there and kill the man. I got a appointment today for my check up so I can get fixed. Mara will kill me if you kill him before he works on me. I, too, am a weak man."

"I wish you'd quit sayin fixed. We ain't dogs."

Ron laughed. "And you ain't fixed."

With that, we walked into the doctor's office.

Old Mabel's eyes got big when she saw me. She give Ron a curt "Sit down." And jerked her head toward me.

Ron obeyed like a new trained puppy and I stomped up to the desk.

Mabel near whispered, "Dr. Cutts is afraid you're gonna sue

him. Are you?"

"I might," I growled.

She nodded her head once. "Well," she sighed, "I reckon I ort to be sued, too. Somehow my sticky note to call you got lost. And what with him a'breakin his arm, he got confused and thought that was your third retest instead of your second."

"Great, just great!" I said a little too loudly. "I cannot believe this crap."

She arched an eyebrow. I didn't usually say nothin even as bad as 'crap'.

"You can bet he said more'n that when he come over here last night and looked at your records. Made me come, too. It weren't no purdy sight."

I rolled my eyes. "I want to talk to him right now."

"I just bet you do. But he has a scheduled appointment to see first." She looked toward Ron.

"He'll swap with me." I turned to Ron. "You don't care if I talk to the good doctor a moment, do you?"

Ron was tryin not to laugh. "By all means. I have all day. Just remember what I asked."

"I won't kill him."

Mabel snorted and told me to sit, so I did, just like my litter mate, Ron.

Dr. Cutts couldn't have apologized more. He admitted gettin his arm broke and all the confusion it caused was the reason my last appointment fell through the cracks. He asked if, "Um, could you, um concentrate enough today for us to do a sperm count?"

I said, why not, so the nurse put me in the little room with everthing and I did what had to be done.

Turns out there was 'one little lively fella' in that count, too.

"So, what you're sayin is I ain't fixed after all." Then I wanted to slap myself upside the head for usin the word 'fixed'.

"Apparently not. By now all rogue sperm should be out of your body. I strongly suggest you still use some form of protection when engagin in sexual activity."

"Are you kiddin me?"

"Oh. Yes, um, well." He mumbled, turnin deep red.

There was a no charge for the visit or retestin.

Ron was no longer in the waitin room when I stormed out, I suppose Mabel wanted him safely tucked away to avoid any ventin in the waitin room.

She's pretty smart, Mabel is.

Bensy's report was as expected. Yes, she was pregnant.

Probably about nine weeks along. I now vividly remembered thinkin how she was glowin and how pale she looked. Made sense. I hadn't seen it for what it was like I had with Monte and the quads, because I thought it couldn't happen again.

Since Lilly Ann was still at preschool, and Monte and the quads was with Mama and Wincy, we was alone for another hour or so. Mama said she reckoned it didn't matter no more if we was alone, nothin monumental would be happenin again, for at least ten months.

Mama thinks she's very funny.

Bensy and me was on the couch, her head on my shoulder.

"You *know* I went back to the doctor. The last thing I asked him was did I need to come back. He said, nope, I got a clean bill of health." I admit it, I was whinin.

"I remember," Bensy said.

I felt like this was all my fault.

"It's not your fault. What is it that little sign says over at Gladys' thirft store? *'God don't make no mistakes'*. This baby was meant to be, that's all there is to it."

"But your body - you was so pleased..."

"Vanity, plain and simple. Charles, do you love me even

217

when I'm pregnant?"

"Lord, Bensy. You know I love you pre-preggers, preggers and post-preggers. I love you all the time."

"Well then, I have to believe you love me no matter how good or bad my figure is. So, my figure will have to come back later."

"But what if you have a bunch of babies again? You might not be so healthy this time."

"Charles, that isn't likely - I mean there was two flukes - one, I dropped two eggs instead of one, which you fertilized quite nicely."

I groaned. She patted my hand.

"Then one of those eggs split three ways. Two flukes, not likely to happen again. And remember, we had two singles before the quads."

"True. I know."

"Plus think of all the baby clothes we have! I ain't got rid of any because I ain't even had time to think about it."

"Yeah, that's good, I guess." I looked at her pleadinly. "We cain't do this again. This has to be it."

"Of course it will be. I'll get a tubal after delivery. I talked to the mid-wife today. She said that wouldn't be a problem, and they'd schedule it for right after delivery. No more babies. We'll have the perfect number seven, just like in the Bible."

My life felt like I was livin biblical proportions, so I reckoned it was a good way to look at it.

Later that afternoon, after I'd picked Lilly Ann up from preschool, I got on my work clothes and went to see what I could help Tate Graham with.

My first few days of 'helpin' him hadn't been too steady, what with the party and the news resultin in a nervous breakdown and a doctor's appointment.

He saw me comin and hollered at me to hold up, he wanted to talk to me a minute.

He clapped me on the back. "How are you?"

"Stunned. Reelin. I dunno. I need one of Uncle Wend's words."

Tate Graham laughed. "I can imagine. But I wanted to congratulate you."

"You'll be the first."

"I figured. Look, Charles. I know this sounds unbelievable,

but Sophia and I would love to be in your shoes."

I looked at him. I saw the sincerity in his eyes.

"Both of us always wanted a large brood of children. But with Sophia's age, the doctors told us to consider ourselves blessed that Andrea was a normal, healthy baby. And we do. We know we're blessed."

"I appreciate the words, Tate Graham. Once I can get past the shock of it all, I know everthing will be all right. Bensy is pretty calm. I'm the one who has lost his mind."

Tate Graham smiled. "Well, if it will make you feel any better, Sophia and I will both feel honored if you will allow us to share your big family. We are thrilled that Andrea can grow up so close to your kids, you know that. One more just makes it merrier, right?"

"Whew. I reckon. Just pray I can move through this maze of feelins. I'm mad at Dr. Cutts for messin up; but I know he didn't mean to. I'm tryin to see it like Bensy sees it; what was meant to be, is. I know she's right. And, Tate Graham, we are gonna need all the help we can get!"

"I promise it to you. Read in your Bible the book of Psalm, chapter 127, verses four and five, you'll see. Now, let's get to work!"

And we did.

****

That night, after everbody was put to bed, Bensy included, I slipped out to the front porch and sat down in the swing, the Bible opened to the Psalms.

The stars was out, the moon was full, and the peepers was singin their song. It was cool enough to almost need a jacket, but not cool enough for me to get up and go back in the house to fetch one.

I sat back and toed the floor so the swing started movin real slow. Sometimes a man needs to be by hisself and think things through. I hardly ever got a chance to do that anymore.

Which may have explained six kids under the age of five, another one on the way, a dog gettin bigger'n a house, and two cats who had claimed imminent domain while we tended their ever whim with an urgency usually saved for servin royalty.

I shook my head, grinnin. I might complain, but I finally had a peaceful feelin about my life.

I heard the screen creak open and saw Dancer openin the door with her snout. She come on out and laid down at my feet with a huff. I reckon everbody needs the front porch sometimes.

I looked around that porch, watchin the shadows sway with the breeze. They wadn't a time in my life that this old porch hadn't served me well. Bensy's life, too, for that matter. We had played in and around and on this porch all our lives. In fact, my daddy and mama had, too, for they was raised across the creek from each other, just like their mamas had been. Our families went way back, and this old porch had seen it all, I reckon.

It was long and deep set, makin it a pleasure to set on in the cool of the evenin, way back before the air conditionin was put in. Generations of bean stringers, banjo pickers and story tellers had come to "set a spell" right where I was.

My life might have challenges, but this, right here, right now, was what a man's heart yearned for.

I started hummin "Amazin Grace" real soft, because I was so full I had to do somethin.

I closed my eyes and just let everthing be. I become still on the inside and felt a joy well up inside me I'd never felt before.

I almost went to sleep, but a baby's cry startled me back to the here and now.

I smiled.

Back to life as I knowed it.

I couldn't hardly wait.

THE END

Uncle Wend's Dictionary

o Arglebargle: A loud argument

o Banjaxed: Broken, ruined, shattered, confounded
o Blalteroon: A senseless babbler, or boaster

o Cacoethes: Irresistible urge to do something inadvisable
o Calumny: Fake charges to harm a reputation
o Cockalorum: A small, haughty man
o Collywobbles: Butterflies in the belly
o Cretinous: (asinine)

o Duplicitous: To fool

o Ersatz: Used as a substitute, usually inferior (an ersatz accent)

o Fudgel (verb): Pretending to work when you're doing nothing at all

o Gelogenic: Tending to produce laughter/ provocative of laughter
o Gobemouche: Gullible
o Godwottery: Nonsense

- Hobbledehoy: Ill manner young boy

- Indubitably: Undoubtedly

- Lagopodous: Like a rabbit's foot (furry footed)
- Loquacious: Talkative.

- Oblectation: The state of being greatly pleased (I spend my days in languid oblectation)
- Obsequious: Fawning over, groveling
- Omnilegent: Reading or having read everything
- Onionmania: Uncontrollable urge to buy things

- Pandiculation: A full body stretch
- Perambulating: Walk or travel through in a leisurely way
- Pettifogger: One who tries to befuddle others with his speech
- Platitudinous: Hebetudinous, stupid, nonsensical
- Polrumptious: Rude, uproarious, overconfident, unruly, disruptive
- PREVARICATE: Speak or act in an evasive manner.

- Quomodocunquizing: Making money any way you can

- Rodomontad : Vainglorious boasting, or bragging, blustering talk, arrogant pretentious

o Smatchet: A contemptible unmannerly person
o Snollygoster: Shrewd unscrulious person usually a politician; someone who can't be trusted
o Solivagant : A lone wonderer
o Soodle: To walk slowly, saunter

o Tatterdemalion: Child in rags
o Titivate: To make oneself look more attractive, or to spruce up and make decorative. (when he says this to Bensy, she adjusts her blouse)

o Ubiquitous: Omnipresent, everywhere

o Zemblanity: The inevitable discovery of what we would rather not know
o Zwodder: Feeling of drowsiness

WHAT OTHERS ARE SAYING ABOUT KATHI'S BOOKS:

On Falling:

> Not since "Love Comes softly", have I enjoyed a Christian romance as much as I have this book. It speaks to everyone that has had struggles in their life, and how God works through the bad times to help you in your walk with Him. This is a compelling story of heartache and triumph that will be treasured by the entire family.

I really enjoyed Falling. It kept me interested in what was going to happen next and it had a lot of substance and meaning about morals and God. It had a happy ending but had a few turns here and there, like real life. I hope she writes more books like this, our society is lacking in morals and this book appeals to all ages.

The book was a well written respectful romance book that anyone would be proud to read.

The book "Falling" told an interesting, beautiful love story without using any vulgarity - what a refreshing concept! I enjoyed reading it from start to finish and have given this book as gifts to friends. They gave a thumbs up as well! Kathi Hill is a gifted writer who uses her talent to uplift others while telling stories that are relevant to today.

This book should be read by every girl - and boy - for that matter - before they begin to date to find out how to have a Christian relationship.

I thought: It must be a great book since James (my husband) never reads anything unless it pertains to his sermon. He came to bed at one a.m. and said he'd read "Falling" in one sitting! So I thought I should read it too! (I did and enjoyed it!)

"Falling" is an enticing book which asks and answers many questions that face young adults today. From the chance meeting of the famous and the wounded through the delicate plan of God, the author weaves a story that is fast paced and delightful for audiences of all ages.

I couldn't wait for the book signing, so I ordered the book off Amazon. From knowing Kathi I wasn't surprised that it was a great book!

My wife purchased the book but I picked it up to read first. I cried in the middle of the story. What a book! I really enjoyed it.

Falling is an excellent, well written book. With humor, Christian values, and a great story-line, it is a book that girls -and guys- will love. Would recommend it to all, especially young adults, for an all-around enjoyable story!

I just happened by the bookstore on the day of Mrs. Hill's book signing for "Falling". Since I work with young people, I purchased a copy and went home to begin reading it over lunch. I sat for one and a half hours without moving until I finished it! What a great book! I rushed back to the bookstore and purchased two more copies, and have been passing those around to "my kids" ever since. Bravo!

A copy of "Falling" was donated to the high school library where I attend school. There has been a constant waiting list to read this book. When I finally got a turn, I could see why! I could picture the characters and scenes just like they were real. I hope she writes another book like this.

Falling is an excellent, well written book. With humor, Christian values, and a great story-line, it is a book that girls -and guys- will love. Would recommend it to all, especially young adults, for an all-around enjoyable story!

What a delightful read!!! Kathi Hill is an outstanding author and leaves her reader begging for more! Loved this read!

A friend told me about this book and i got it. I LOVE this book!!! It was a fast read but a wonderful story! i hope to see more from this author! :)

ON: **The Crow and The Wind**:

This book is a great book for little kids because of the simple story line and wonderful illustrations. But it has a deeper meaning that my 11 year old classroom really discussed, as we are studying symbolism. I recommend this to any parent or teacher who wants to get across the idea that there is someone bigger than us!

This book is a must read for both young and old! A beautiful creation and the author has a great idea of how to get through to people and share the beauty of God. The drawings alone are worth the purchase to see! Awesome book.

The Crow and The Wind is a wonderful book for the child who hears it and the adult who reads it aloud! Both will be blessed by the content of the message and the detail of the illustrations. It's a book that belongs on every bedside table to be shared at bedtime. It will ease the troubles of the day by reminding readers that there is Someone bigger than us who is in charge!

The Crow and the Wind is a children's book. Or is it? This book can be enjoyable and meaningful to Children of all ages. For anyone who still has an imagination and a belief in things not-seen. Actually it is love story about a crow and the wind. They find each other and ultimately God the Creator. The illustrations by David Hill only add to its charm.

The Crow and The Wind is a wonderful little children's book with a great big message! Kathi Harper Hill captures the reader and any little listener within earshot as she takes the crow on a journey of discovery. The beautiful illustrations provide the reader with colorful imagery as the story of God's presence, love and power are told. Hill's words are teaching and the lessons learned are indeed blessings of affirmation!

I enjoyed reading this story even though I don't have small ones. The story reminds us that we can stray from out creator. Then circumstances lead us back to the fold. Well written and beautifully illustrated. I loved the book. I recommend the book for middle schoolers. A great edition to a child's Christian library.

This book takes a child back to an earlier and more rural time. It can be enjoyed by a child for its' visual appeal and its' very positive message. The group of children to whom I read was all attentive and was stimulated to ask many questions.

One Old Crow's Journey to the Truth: In an enchanting mix of old-time Appalachian religion, George MacDonald, and C. S. Lewis, Kathi and David Hill tell a smart and engaging tale of one old crow's journey to the Truth. You couldn't own a better bedtime story.

This is a lovely book, with a gentle humor and beautiful illustrations. I was enchanted and have shared it with my friends.

The Crow and The Wind is such a wonderful book. The story is great. I love the illustrations. I have already recommended this book to several people. This is a "must have" book!

I bought this book for my grandson. We have thoroughly enjoyed reading it together. He loved the story and the illustrations. I'm sure that it will be one book that we will read over and over again. Would highly recommend this book.

ON: **<u>OUT ON A LIMB OF THE FAMILY TREE</u>**:

This one is my favorite book that Kathi has written so far, I think!

Can't wait for my friends to read this! All us "older" women remember and everyone is in a hurry to read this one!

I was raised to talk like this, and my mother still does. Brought back a lot of fond memories.

This book was so good! I could just see Missouri sitting on the porch. They should make a movie out of this book!

This book captures the heart and soul of the rural south. The language is words and phrases I grew up hearing from my grandparents and parents. Some words I still use today. Kathi captures the essence of the love and support that strong Southern women have given their families over the last 200 years. Missouri and Kizzie are great reminders of my granny and her sister. Another great read from a great Southern author! Even the Yankees will love it!

This a fabulous book about small town life in the Appalachian Mountains! Kathi Harper Hill brings the characters to life and I felt like I was right back in my Grandmothers Kitchen! It left me feeling good and wanting more!

Southern spoken here...

Were you lucky enough to grow up in a small town? In the

50s and 60s? In the south? In the foothills of the Appalachians? With lots of close kin? If so, you'll feel totally at home with this charming book about family, bossy as they are. If not, you'll learn what it is like to be so blessed...So put down that arn, put on your earbobs and Sunday dress, and go git yourself a copy of this charming tale!

Out On A Limb Of The Family Tree is an excellent book about Appalachian life including the language. Kathi did an outstanding job with the terminology. This book grabs your attention and keeps it. It is well written, descriptive to the point of you being surprised when you stop reading and realize you're not sitting on the porch with Missouri. It makes you laugh, cry and times that you feel like you lost your own dear friend that moved on to Heaven. No matter if your southern or not everyone can identify with some character in this story. I thought she was writing about my aunties. Must read.

Kathi Harper Hill is one of the best authors I have ever read. I couldn't put the book down it was so good. I laughed and I cried throughout the whole book. I felt like I was actually a part of this "southern" family. I loved how Missouri never lost her faith in God and how she had raised her family to have that same faith in God. It is a must read for everyone.

A book you can't put down. I didn't except the range of emotions I felt, from laughing till it hurt to tears of sadness. This is a great story one I would recommend to everyone.

I just finished "Out On a Limb of the Family Tree". What a treat! If you grew up in the southern Appalachian Mountains, you will recognize the characters as your granny, your papa, your aunts, your elderly neighbors. You will laugh and you will cry. You will rejoice with them and mourn with them. If you didn't grow up in this area, do yourself a favor and read the book anyway. The "belly-laughs" are many, the joy is contagious and you'll get a new outlook on life! The author hit one out of the park with this book!

"Out on a Limb of the Family Tree" is about Appalachian family stories and is full of some of the funniest stuff I've ever read! But it also made me wistful for the days when Appalachia was not fading away into the modern day world.

If you are from the Appalachian Mountains or the South, READ THIS BOOK!

"Out on a Limb of the Family Tree" was the kind of book you think is real and are startled to look up from a page and find out you aren't "there". Sometimes I think she was looking in my granny's windows and taking notes!

I just loved the people in this book, especially the little old women. I will forever hold these people dear to my heart!

On: Signs from God:

She needs to contact those guys that do the movies from Albany, Georgia. This would make a great Christian movie.

I couldn't stop reading this book! I just loved it!

What a cute book. It made me laugh out loud!

It's as good a book I've ever read in this genre.

Overall, I found this to be a very good, well-written book. I believe Christian girls of all ages will like it; even some men may enjoy it. It's funny, romantic and exciting; a good, modern book that will warm many people's hearts. From the start the book caught my interest and it never ceased to intrigue me.

Another wonderful book by Kathi Hill. Signs From God is a beautiful love story not only between a man and woman but involved love of God, family, friends, two babies and a dog as well. I did not want to put it down and enjoyed every page. Kathi is such a gifted author and she has a way of getting the reader so involved with the characters that you feel like you know them personally.

I loved this wonderful piece of literature! I've ordered all of Kathi Hill's books and haven't been disappointed! I love her fun, easy to follow stories!

"You won't want to put it down". The book is amazing, inspiring and heartwarming. Kathi's love of animals also comes across in her writing as you will find out. This is a "must read" for everyone.

"Signs from God" is my favorite book that Hill has written so far. It's a contemporary

novel, and even though I'm not from the south, I was able to enjoy it thoroughly.

Kathi Harper Hill is a talented writer. Signs from God is another one of her excellent reads. I was drawn right into the story and just couldn't put it down till it was finished. So ready for her next book.

If you love dogs, you'll love the book. Interesting story, engaging from the get go.

"The Christmas Closet and Other Works"

Mrs. Hill came to our school and read the first story, "The Christmas Closet" to our fifth grade class. They loved it, and so did I! I was a Roy Rogers fan and it brought back my own little boy childhood. What a great story!

I purchased this book because I thought it would be a good Christmas book for Christians. And though most of the stories are, and all the poems are about the Christ Child, the first story was not. I have never taught my children to believe in Santa Claus, nor was I taught to do so. Nevertheless, the story made me cry and then smile when the terrible problem was repaired.

I am not of the Christian faith, but two of my children's teachers are, so I purchased this book as gifts to them at Christmas. They both loved it and thanked me over and over!

"The Christmas Closet and Other Works" was a great gift for all the people in my office. Everyone seemed to have a different favorite, and I'll think I'll buy a few more copies next year for some friends.

On "The Year of Nine: *Where the Rain Begins:*

"Gifted Southern Author Kathi Harper Hill tells us an adventure filled tale about nine year Tansy's life in a small town in the North Georgia Mountains. From a peeping-tom to red measles to seeing the ocean for the first time, 1963 is Tansy's year to remember, lots of ups and downs, highs and lows, all told with a southern sensibility and twang. A must read for those loving a good solid story about growing up in the south. *The Best of Ellijay, Blue Ridge & jasper Funpaper*

"Hill has created a highly enjoyable read, which in turn induces sidesplitting laughter and poignant reflection. The novel's young protagonist sees the world through the refreshingly clear lens of youth and her observations about the issues of the turbulent 1960s and growing older are spot on. By the end of the first chapter, I felt a kinship with the characters and was reminded of several time-worn, long-forgotten memories from my own "year of nine." Readers are sure to enjoy this funny, charming story of a rich childhood spent in the mountains of north Georgia."

Whitney Crouch is a staff writer at the Times-Courier newspaper in Ellijay, Ga., She has won several writing awards from the Georgia Press Association for feature writing, education coverage and humorous column.

The Year of Nine: Where the Rain Begins, by Kathi Harper Hill, is a rare find – a charming and genuine glimpse into the small-town Appalachian life of yesteryear, through the eyes of 9-year-old Tansy Corbin. Tansy's world is a small North Georgia town shaped like grandmother's mixing bowl, where everyone had a garden and nearly everyone had an indoor   toilet.

In her the sixth book, Kathi Harper Hill draws deep from her experience in small-town Appalachia and from her rich storytelling skills to paint an authentic portrait of simpler times. The summer of 1963 was an innocent time and the last summer that things stayed the same for Tansy. It was the first time her Mama ever spoke to her like a grown up. Harper Hill uses Tansy's wit and innocence wisdom to introduce Mama, Daddy, G-Papa, G-Tansy, Tink, and a host of family and friends. She reminds us of the child-like wonder and excitement (and fear and worry) of a vacation to the ocean or a trip to the zoo in Atlanta and of the sadness of losing   someone   we   love.

Kathi Harper Hill is one of my favorite Southern writers. She's witty and wise and The Year of Nine: Where the Rain Begins, is the kind of warm, old-fashioned novel you will want recommend to your friends.

Tim Rice, DMin, LPC, author of *Homeschool Psychology: Preparing Christian Homeschool Students for Psychology*

101 and *Psychology: A Christian Perspective, High School Edition* teaches psychology online live.

In The Year of Nine Where the Rain Begins, Kathi Harper Hill gives us a beautifully written and satisfying novel. Set during the early Sixties in a small town in north Georgia, it is the coming of age story of Tansy Corbin as she navigates her ninth year and realizes for the first time that life is change, and that change is hard. There is nothing better than a simple story told well, and Hill has succeeded in doing just that. Her attention to the nuances of life in the rural South will make readers long for a time and a place in the world that is no more. —Raymond L, Atkins, is an award winning author whose work includes: *Sweetwater Blues, Camp Redemption, Sorrow Wood and The Front Porch Prophet.*

The Year of Nine: Where the Rain Begins is a delightful book that allows the reader to drift back to simpler times in a very special place that simply no longer exists. For those lucky enough to have grown up in a place like Ellijay, you will recognize many similarities to your own childhood. Kathi Harper Hill brilliantly manages to breathe life into the dear and quirky characters of this novel, and she does so with such a sweet innocence that harkens back to that time and place. I found myself laughing out loud, and at the same time, I actually needed a handkerchief more than once to wipe away tears. Kathi Harper Hill has a knack of telling a story in such a way that she captures the reader from the very beginning! She always seems to leave you wanting just one more paragraph or just one more page! The book is a wonderful look at the innocence of childhood, and in a way, the innocence of small town America before the tumultuous changes that would come in November 1963. It is another 5 STAR product from a gifted writer with great stories to tell!

Very enjoyable read. I grew up out in the country in the same county as Tansy. I recognize several of the characters in the book which just made it more interesting to me. I remember the town as Tansy describes it and was in her granddaddy's store many times. I always got to go to town on Saturdays with my grandpa and her granddaddy's store was always our last stop as we were leaving town. Although I was the "country mouse" and she was the "town mouse" our childhoods were very similar. Family, extended family, friends. and church was the center of our universe. But this is a book that anyone would enjoy, even if you did not have the childhood of Tansy. Kathi is a great storyteller and captures the language and feel for the innocent times before we were old enough to pay attention to the news of Viet Nam, racial tension, and Soviet fear that was on the nightly news. It was a time of fun, games, freedom, and no fear of your neighbors or even most strangers. If you lived in town or out in the country you could play outside from daylight till dark and never worry about anything bad happening to you. It truly was the best of times!

If you grew up in a small town where everyone knew everyone, or if you only wish you had grown up in that place, you will love "The Year of Nine". Hill captures the thoughts and images of childhood in a way that will transport her readers back in time to a simpler, purer way of life. What a joy it was to return to a setting where 9 year old children were still innocent and life was explained by caring, responsible adults. "The Year of Nine" caused me to remember that friendships forged in childhood in a safe, protected place will last a lifetime! Buy it, read it, savor it!

I live in the area this book was written about and I really enjoyed it. I like that she wrote it from the child's point of view and to me that really put you in that place and time. It was so easy to picture my town in this time period. She captured the sense of community and the spirit of our little town perfectly. Although times have changed, the people in this area are still much like the characters in her book. I look forward to reading more of her work.

What a heartwarming, delightful, easy read!! I literally laughed out loud throughout the book. I too grew up in the South in the 50's and 60's. It was indeed a simpler/safer time. I have recommended The Year of Nine: Where the Rain Begins to several friends and co-workers. I look forward to reading more of Kathi Harper Hill's books.

This is a wonderful summer read. Being from South Ga. and visiting this small North Ga. hamlet every summer growing up the stories give a bird's eye view of the culture from within.

Really enjoyed this book, wonderful childhood memories. Kathi Harper Hill is a true storyteller..

Kathi Hill is one of my all time favorite authors. She writes from the heart. Love, *love* this book

Nostalgic and funny. If you grew up in a small town in the 60's, you'll enjoy this read.

Kathi Harper Hill has lived in the North Georgia Mountains all her life. She has been writing since the age of ten. After taking early retirement as a professional in the mental health field, she began devoting more time to her craft. Her stories, told with southern humor, focus mainly on relationships, and how relationships force growth in the characters.

Besides loving to write (and read), her other interests include teaching Bible classes, interior design, and music. Kathi has been a soloist since the age of fourteen.

Hill is the author of six books. Her first, "Falling", was published in 2009, and is directed toward young adults who enjoy reading romance. Her children's book, "The Crow and The Wind" *a little book about a Big God,* was first runner up in the mid-child division at the 2011 **Georgia Author of the Year Awards**. Hill has been the recipient of numerous awards for her short stories over the years. One of these winning stories appears in "The Christmas Closet and Other Works". Her other three books are novels, "Signs from God", "Out on a Limb of the Family Tree", and "The Year of Nine: *Where the Rain Begins*".

She and her husband, David, (who does illustrations in her books), live in a Victorian cottage with their daughter, Anna Kate, and current menagerie of pets: The Great White Cats: Frost and Eli; Anna Kate's cat, Mimi, joins the fray; American Bulldog, Bonnie; and one lone fish who goes by the name of Fin.

CPSIA information can be obtained
at www.ICGtesting.com
Printed in the USA
FSOW02n1917291016
26709FS